The Howling Castle

The huge, iron-studded front door groaned open to reveal a tall, thin man, silhouetted by the cold light that poured out from within.

The man stood silently, watching the twins approach. It was only when they reached the bottom of the stone staircase that he took a single step forward. Hands clasped in front of him, almost as if in prayer, he greeted them with a tight-lipped smile.

Adam and Lana stopped dead. They were both thinking exactly the same thing, but only Adam spoke.

'Dracula!' he breathed.

Books by Steve Rogers

Fright Night: The Shrieking Stones
Fright Night: The Howling Castle

The Howling Castle

STEVE ROGERS

PUFFIN

PUFFIN BOOKS

Published by the Penguin Group
Penguin Books Ltd, 80 Strand, London WC2R ORL, England
Penguin Group (USA) Inc., 375 Hudson Street, New York, New York 10014, USA
Penguin Group (Canada), 90 Eglinton Avenue East, Suite 700, Toronto, Ontario, Canada M4P 2Y3
(a division of Pearson Penguin Canada Inc.)
Penguin Ireland, 25 St Stephen's Green, Dublin 2, Ireland (a division of Penguin Books Ltd)
Penguin Group (Australia), 250 Camberwell Road, Camberwell, Victoria 3124, Australia
(a division of Pearson Australia Group Pty Ltd)
Penguin Books India Pvt Ltd, 11 Community Centre, Panchsheel Park, New Delhi – 110 017, India
Penguin Group (NZ), 67 Apollo Drive, Rosedale, North Shore 0632, New Zealand
(a division of Pearson New Zealand Ltd)
Penguin Books (South Africa) (Pty) Ltd, 24 Sturdee Avenue, Rosebank,
Johannesburg 2196, South Africa

Penguin Books Ltd, Registered Offices: 80 Strand, London WC2R ORL, England

puffinbooks.com

First published 2008
1

Text copyright © CPI Hothouse, 2008
All rights reserved

Set in Baskerville MT
Typeset by Palimpsest Book Production Limited, Grangemouth, Stirlingshire
Made and printed in England by Clays Ltd, St Ives plc

British Library Cataloguing in Publication Data
A CIP catalogue record for this book is available from the British Library

ISBN: 978-0-141-32373-2

www.greenpenguin.co.uk

With special thanks to Simon Forward

1

The train clanked noisily away, puffing out a billowing cloud of steam that rolled back to smother the small group of passengers. For a moment, they all just stood there, surrounded by bags and suitcases, as if hoping that the steam would clear and reveal that their first impressions had been mistaken, and that they hadn't been left on a lonely platform in the middle of nowhere.

Even Lana felt a creeping sense of unease as details of their surroundings began to emerge. The 'station' was more like a ramshackle shed perched on the side of the railway track. The moss-clad bricks and rotting woodwork glistened in the light of an almost full moon. Beyond the tracks, a gloomy pine forest stretched up the slopes of one of the many steep mountains that loomed over them.

After a long flight, followed by two rail journeys, she was suffering from jet-lag, train-lag and just about every other kind of lag, so she was wary of her imagination playing tricks on her. But she reluctantly had to admit that this place definitely *looked* spooky.

Lana shivered. Life had been a lot simpler when she didn't believe in ghosts.

Only a few weeks earlier, on location in Ireland, Lana had not only met a real ghost – a mischievous Irish spirit called Fergus – she had also narrowly escaped becoming one herself. But even though she could no longer deny the existence of the supernatural, that didn't mean she went looking for ghosts round every corner. She left that to her twin brother, Adam. He was already snooping around the deserted platform, peering through broken windows as if expecting a phantom to leap out at any moment.

'Wow! This is brilliant!'

'It's only some run-down old station,' sniffed Lana. 'And I don't care what it looks like. I just want to get to bed.'

'Don't we all.'

That sharp voice could only belong to Angela Clancy, the producer of Uncle Larry's TV show

Fright Night and bossy-boots extraordinaire. Ever since he had heard they were coming to Romania, Adam had taken to calling her 'Bride of Dracula'. But only when she was a safe distance away. Everyone knew Angela had eyes in the back of her head, but she also had ears that could pick up the slightest mention of her name, no matter how quietly it was whispered.

'Well,' continued Angela, 'the van should be waiting for us in the car park, so the *sooner* we get outside the *better*. Come along, everybody!'

The twins' Uncle Larry picked up his own bags and set off after Angela with a spring in his step, sporting an eager expression that somehow managed to make his worry-lined face seem almost young again.

'This is fantastic, isn't it, children?' he declared as the twins hauled on their backpacks. 'Enormous potential! I can feel it in my bones. You mark my words, we're going to find something truly special here.'

Uncle Larry had been getting more and more excited ever since Angela had announced that their destination for the latest episode of *Fright Night* was this remote region of Romania. He'd reached fever pitch when the final leg of their journey had turned out to be along an isolated little branch line, where they still operated a steam engine, presumably for the benefit of tourists. Except Lana hadn't seen any tourists. In fact, she hadn't seen any other passengers at all. But then – she glanced at her watch with a sigh that turned into a yawn – it was very, very late.

Behind them, the rest of the crew brought up the rear, groaning and struggling under the combined weight of their personal luggage and all the essential TV equipment – cameras, microphones, and assorted tripods and cables. Lana sympathized with their quiet grumbles.

Emerging from the station, they found themselves in a car park as deserted as the platform. Several of the crew glanced nervously at Angela. As usual, she had taken charge of the whole journey, directing them through the airports at both ends, and assigning everybody their seats like a horribly strict teacher organizing a school trip. So the idea of something not happening according to her carefully prepared schedule was unlikely to go down well.

'Where on *earth* is that blasted van?'

Uncle Larry cast an eye over the crew and their collective load. 'Perhaps they're having trouble finding one vehicle big enough to accommodate us all,' he suggested nervously.

Angela shot him one of her famous withering glares – piercing enough to penetrate armour.

'Nonsense. I arranged for the hotel to send a large van. I shall be having words with the Count. He's the owner, so he's *supposed* to be in charge.'

'Look!' called Adam, pointing towards a pair of lights approaching from a distance. 'That could be it coming now.'

'Whatever it is, it's far too slow to be a van,' said Lana.

Before long the reason for the lights' leisurely pace became obvious: an open carriage drawn by a pair of fine black horses emerged from the gloom. A couple of lanterns served as the vehicle's headlamps. Eventually, it drew into the car park and the driver reined the horses to a halt and jumped down.

Clad in a long, dark coat, much of his face was muffled by a scarf, and his eyes were hidden under the broad brim of his hat. Slowly, he walked over towards the crew, leather boots creaking, and stopped in front of Angela. He tugged his scarf down, revealing swarthy features and a drooping moustache.

'Welcome to Wallachia. My name is Benedikte,' he said. Benedikte's accent was almost as thick as his bushy eyebrows, but he grinned widely as he caught sight of the twins, and doffed his hat politely. 'I will take you to Castle Dragomir.'

Adam took a deep breath. First a steam train, now a horse-drawn carriage. He suddenly felt that they had not only arrived in a foreign country, but also slipped back in time.

2

Riding along in the open air, Lana felt a little like Cinderella. Or how she imagined Cinderella would have felt if she'd still been inside her carriage when it had turned back into a pumpkin. With all eight members of the crew crammed inside, it was such a tight squeeze that she was in danger of being squashed to a pulp. To make the ride even less comfortable, Lana had the bad luck to be next to Angela – pressed up much closer than she would ever have willingly chosen.

'Can't we ride up front?' Adam asked, almost as soon as they were on their way.

'No, no, no,' replied Benedikte with a low chuckle. 'Guests sit in the back. Only servants ride up front. Too dangerous.'

'Now, children, I know it's a little, um, cosy,'

said Uncle Larry, 'but remember, Angela had to trim down the crew considerably to allow you two to come along. Besides,' he added cheerfully, gesturing at the passing scenery, 'this all adds to the adventure. Something to write about to your mum and dad.'

Lana didn't rate her chances of fitting all her current complaints into a single letter. Assuming she could even find a post office in this wild and remote spot.

'It's certainly eerie,' admitted Angela. 'Although we could do with some *snow* to really set the mood. It's not the season for it, but perhaps we'll be lucky.'

Lana groaned inwardly. It was typical of Angela to wish for bad weather. She claimed it added 'atmosphere'. Lana had to remind herself that they weren't on holiday, and she had to admit that when you were in the business of making spooky TV shows, atmosphere counted for a lot.

In fact, it was a beautiful night. Only a few smears of cloud drifted across the stars and lightly smudged the face of the moon. The surrounding peaks and valleys lay under a great lunar spotlight; hedgerows marked out fields like dense stitching on a vast patchwork quilt. Lana looked forward to admiring the view in the morning, transformed by daylight and eyes that had benefited from plenty of sleep.

The road wound on, leaving behind pastures filled with sheep, and rising into the shadows of the forest. The thickening trees blocked out the moonlight. For some minutes they drove in silence. Then, suddenly, something caught Lana's eye, far off through the trees: a pale glow that bathed the trunks and branches with flickering light.

'What's that?' she said, pointing.

'Campfire,' said Benedikte. 'Probably children from the village – making trouble!' he added, with a wink at the twins.

'Couldn't it be a Romany camp?' asked Adam. 'I've heard that the Romany people live all over this part of Europe.'

Benedikte shook his head. 'Not any more. Not in these lands anyway. Here, they vanished long ago. Once Romany people were as common as wolves in these parts, but now . . .'

Angela shifted nervously in her seat. 'Wolves? Nobody mentioned *anything* about wolves.'

'Oh yes,' replied Benedikte cheerfully. 'These

mountains, they are ruled by the wolves more than any man.' The coachman fell quiet, as though allowing the night to tell the rest of the story, but the only sound was the *clip-clop* of hooves and the faint grinding of wheels on the poorly surfaced road. 'But beware. Speak of the devil and he will appear.'

'Excuse me?' said Uncle Larry.

Benedikte nodded to the other side of the road. Suddenly, silently, dozens of grey shapes slipped out from the trees, almost as though they had been lying in ambush.

Wolves.

The pack halted by the roadside, eyes shining as they sniffed the air. Then, as Adam and Lana watched, they broke into a steady lope, pouring up the hill after the carriage.

'Is that *normal* behaviour?' Angela asked, her voice squeaking slightly. Everyone looked to Benedikte, but the driver just shrugged his shoulders.

'Well, are they dangerous?'

'They look dangerous,' said Adam, who was keeping his eyes on the animals. As the beasts quickened their pace, several of them bared their fangs – and growled. 'Weird. Most wolves are more afraid of humans than we are of them.'

'They will leave us alone once we get out of the forest,' said Benedikte confidently.

'Then perhaps you could get us out of the forest a bit *quicker*,' suggested Angela, doing her best to conceal what sounded like fear under a nervous smile.

Benedikte glanced back. The wolves were close now, just a few metres behind the carriage. 'I will see what I can do.' He flicked the reins and cracked his whip. '*Hyah! Hyah!*'

The horses immediately quickened their pace from a trot to a canter. Adam and Lana looked behind, expecting to see the wolf pack dropping away. But the wolves seemed to take the change of speed as encouragement. Gleefully, they leaped to the chase.

'We should get the cameras out,' suggested Adam. 'This would be pretty amazing footage.'

'No, that's perfectly all right,' Angela told him tightly, staring dead ahead. 'We can stick to my *original* plan for an atmospheric opening shot of the castle, thank you very much.'

Now they were racing up the steep, winding

road, weaving around shadowy bends, through the murky forest. The wolves threw themselves eagerly after their prey. They were so close, Lana could see muscles rippling under their silver-grey fur. Uncle Larry yelped as his wig slipped over his eyes, blinding him. He reached up to hold it in place – as a wolf snapped at the side of the carriage, right where his hand had just been. Angela let out a stifled scream.

'Better get a move on!' yelled Adam.

'*Hyah! Hyah!*' Benedikte lashed the whip again.

The trees sped past in a blur and Adam and Lana – along with everyone else – were shaken roughly about. If they hadn't been so tightly crammed into their seats, they would have been thrown out. The wolves seemed to delight in their panic, panting keenly as they fought to stay with the carriage, their eyes blazing even brighter in the darkness.

Then, as the carriage rounded another bend, the hill steepened still further. The twins glanced at each other, afraid the exhausted horses might slacken their pace. But Benedikte wouldn't allow it. He lashed them again. '*Hyah! Hyah!*'

The coachman drove the horses into a mad

gallop for the gateway they could just make out at the top of the road. Stone gargoyles perched on top of each gatepost, but despite their twisted, demonic features they were a welcome sight. As the carriage sped past them, Adam and Lana looked behind again. Finally, the wolves were slowing.

Still panting, tongues lolling between gleaming fangs, the animals dropped to a walk. But their eyes gazed longingly after the carriage, watching Adam and Lana, it seemed, all the way up the drive until they disappeared from view. A mournful howl echoed through the night behind them.

'Castle Dragomir!' proclaimed Benedikte as he reined in the horses and brought them to a smart halt. Despite the terrifying carriage ride, he sounded like a bus driver announcing one of his more routine destinations. 'Fun ride, huh?'

The enormous castle looked like something from a dark fairy tale. Ivy clung reluctantly to crumbling walls and spires, seeming as if it would rather have been somewhere else. The moon edged the rooftops and high battlements with an eerie blue glow, giving the building the sickly look of something recently dead. Most of the windows were dark, and where light did shine out, it seemed cold and hard rather than warm and inviting.

'Wow! This gets better and better!' Adam nudged his sister and pointed up at the ancient facade of brick and stone. 'It's the ultimate haunted castle!'

Lana rolled her eyes. 'I'm just glad we got here in one piece. That man drives like a maniac.'

'It was pretty cool,' laughed Adam.

'Pretty dangerous, more like. Now all I want to do is go to bed.'

Adam smirked. 'Assuming you can sleep. A place like this will be crawling with creepy goings-on, I'll bet.'

Lana tutted and shook her head. She looked back at the carriage, where the crew were unloading the luggage. Angela had paused from supervising it all in her usual stern and fussy way to cast an eagle eye over the castle. She sniffed, but spoke with a rare tone of satisfaction. 'Yes, well, this *certainly* has qualities we can work with. We had all just better hope we can conjure up something as *special* as we managed in Ireland.'

'Can we go in now?' prompted Lana impatiently.

'Not until everything is unloaded and –'

In the distance, a wolf howled.

Angela jumped nervously and shot a worried look back down the drive in the direction of the gates. 'On second thoughts, yes. Let's go.' She grabbed her own designer suitcase and set off towards the main door of the castle at something like a run.

Adam and Lana glanced back, wondering whether they should wait for Uncle Larry, but he seemed to be busy rooting through a pile of luggage, looking for something.

As the twins walked towards the flight of steep stone stairs that led up to the hotel entrance where Angela was ringing the bell impatiently, the carriage finally pulled away. With the light from the carriage-lanterns gone, the shadows in the castle courtyard deepened threateningly. Lana frowned.

'Something up, sis?'

'Probably nothing.' She looked at her brother, who had fallen into step beside her. 'But don't you think it's a bit odd that no one's come out to meet us?'

Adam smiled, his eyes widening. 'Oh, so now who's imagining creepy goings-on?'

'No,' insisted Lana. 'I should have known you'd try to make it sound sinister. I just mean it's not very good service. I know it's late, but we are expected, after all.'

As Lana was pondering this minor mystery and wondering whether Angela might complain about the lack of a warmer welcome, the huge, iron-studded front door groaned open to reveal a tall, thin man, silhouetted by the cold light that poured out from within.

The man stood silently, watching the twins approach. It was only when they reached the bottom of the stone staircase that he took a single step forward. Hands clasped in front of him, almost as if in prayer, he greeted them with a tight-lipped smile.

Adam and Lana stopped dead. They were both thinking exactly the same thing, but only Adam spoke.

'Dracula!' he breathed.

3

'Dracula?' said the man in the doorway, as though savouring the word in his mouth and liking the taste. Tall and thin, he had a gaunt face, and his dark hair was combed so severely back from his high forehead that it seemed to pull the skin taut over his skull. He had coal-dark eyes set in deep hollows, but he smiled at the twins, amused. 'Thank you. I am flattered. I am Count Dragos Dragomir, owner of this hotel.'

Adam lowered his eyes. He certainly hadn't meant his comment to be heard.

'Please, don't mind them,' said Angela. 'The boy sees ghosts and monsters everywhere. The girl is at least *slightly* more sensible.'

'Ah, it is no harm. I am not in the least offended.' The Count graced Adam with a thin smile that somehow made him feel more awkward than ever. 'You are here to find ghosts, are you not? A sixth sense will come in handy. And twins often have strange powers . . .' The Count's eyes flashed for a moment before he turned back to Angela. 'Besides, children's imaginations like to run wild. And things that run wild are best given their freedom. If they are cornered, they may turn around and bite your hand, yes?'

'Um, yes, I suppose so,' said Angela, shooting Adam a look that strongly suggested that he'd better not think of doing any such thing.

Adam shrugged. *He* had no plans to go biting anyone. But he wasn't sure the same could be said of the Count. Adam had already noted that the man smiled with his mouth closed, keeping his teeth hidden. Was that just his manner or was he being careful to conceal a set of sharp vampire fangs?

'In our country,' the Count continued, 'we do not understand why your English writer Bram Stoker based his famous vampire on Vlad Dracula. Here in Romania, Vlad is a hero, a man who defended this nation against medieval invaders. So, you see, I am truly honoured you should call me by that name.'

Adam wasn't sure he wanted a late-night history lesson from this strange man. All he was certain of was that the Count gave him the creeps. They would have to keep an eye on him while they were here. Although Lana would probably laugh at his suspicions as soon as he mentioned them to her.

The Count clicked his heels and gave a modest bow. 'But forgive me, do come in. You must have had a long journey. You look tired.'

'Yes, we just ran into some of your local *wildlife*,' muttered Angela with a shudder.

'Wolves,' Lana explained. 'Loads of them.'

'Ah yes, the wolves are many in these parts, but they are not the worst –'

'Indeed,' interrupted Angela. 'We were *very* intrigued by your claim that this is the most haunted castle in Romania.'

'Oh, that is most certainly true, I guarantee you,' replied the Count, smiling. 'My family have owned the castle for centuries, although I myself have only recently returned to live here. But already I have seen things within these walls that would make your blood run cold: strange figures in the corridors, the sound of sobbing in the night and objects moving around the castle of their own accord . . .'

Adam's eyes gleamed. Back in England, he'd been thrilled when Angela had passed on the news about the ghosts that supposedly haunted Castle Dragomir. Lana was less impressed. The Count was probably very good at telling tall tales for the tourists. Still, there *was* something sinister about him – and their encounter with the wolves hadn't helped to settle her nerves.

'But forgive my manners,' said the Count as the rest of the crew straggled over. 'I should be offering my guests more than ghost stories. I am afraid you have missed dinner, but I would be happy to wake the chef and have him prepare you some refreshments.'

'Thank you, that *won't* be necessary,' said Angela, before anyone else could voice their opinion on the matter. 'If you could just have someone show us to our rooms.'

'Of course, of course. Lucian!'

A stooped, grey-haired man wearing an impeccably smart gold-buttoned jacket appeared at the Count's elbow.

'This is Lucian, the hotel manager. He will see to your every need. We are privileged to have television people here as our guests. I hope we will create a good impression.'

Angela favoured the Count with a tired smile. 'Well, I must say, I like what I have seen so far.'

'Not sure I do,' muttered Adam.

The Count peered down at him. 'What was that, young man?'

'Adam!' hissed Lana.

'I was just saying that if you could tell us our room number, we could probably find it ourselves,' said Adam, doing his best to ignore Angela's narrow-eyed scowl. 'And get out of everyone's way.'

The Count smiled thinly. 'I would not dream of it. The castle is like a maze. You might get lost – and never found.'

Lana shuddered, but the Count gave a dry chuckle. 'Forgive me. I am joking of course. Now, if you will excuse me, I have other matters that demand my attention.' He bowed and walked off towards a small stable block on the far side of the lawn.

'Now, why's he going to the stables at this time of night?' mused Adam.

'Who cares? Why did you have to say you didn't like the look of him?' scolded Lana as Lucian ushered them through the door, while

Angela paused to bark some instructions at Uncle Larry. 'We've only been here five minutes and you're already getting us in trouble.'

'Leave off, Lana. I bet you thought the same when you saw him.'

'You can't assume someone's a vampire just because of the way they look.'

'Careful,' said Adam. 'I was right about ghosts existing.'

Lana sighed. Her brother had been teasing her mercilessly since their trip to Ireland and their encounters with Fergus and the ghostly witch, Ghian. 'Yes, but just because ghosts exist, that doesn't mean that every other type of mythical monster does too.'

Adam snorted. Lana couldn't deny the existence of ghosts any more. As far as he was concerned, that meant she should be more open-minded to other spooky possibilities. Vampires included.

'You just wait. Uncle Larry'll take one look at the Count and think the same as me. Ghosts aren't going to be the creepiest thing we find here −'

'Wow!' interrupted Lana as they stepped into the entrance hall.

Spacious, with a worn flagstone floor and a ceiling almost dizzyingly high, the hall was dominated by the grand, blue-carpeted staircase at one end. Everywhere else – the walls, the desk, the banister on the staircase – gleamed with highly polished wood. Huge portraits stared down from the walls, their old-fashioned occupants seeming perfectly at home in the ancient surroundings.

Lucian planted himself behind the main desk, ready to take charge of checking in. He handed Lana a large iron key. 'You are in Room 124. If you wait just a moment, I will show you the way.'

Adam picked up a glossy colour brochure from the desk. The cover showed Castle Dragomir dramatically silhouetted against a stormy sky, complete with forks of lightning. Right across the top, words had been printed to look like dripping blood:

Castle Dragomir, the most haunted castle in Romania – *AS SEEN ON TV!*

'Well, they seem pretty sure we're going to find some ghosts,' he muttered to Lana, flicking through the pages. 'Hey, cool – it says here that all the rooms have free Internet access.'

Lucian sighed. 'Yes, there is work still to be done on some parts of the castle but we have all the latest technology here.'

'Great.'

'Why?' hissed Lana. 'What can you possibly want with the Internet at this time of night?'

'What's it to you? I'll be quiet. I'm not going to keep you awake.'

'You'd better not,' she warned him, frowning.

'So, both you children know about technology, yes?' enquired Lucian. 'That is why they hired you for the TV show?'

Adam laughed. 'We're not hired.'

'No, they don't pay us. We're not really part of the crew,' explained Lana, also enjoying the joke. 'Our uncle is looking after us while our parents are away. They're scientists, working at the South Pole.'

'Uncle Larry is the presenter,' added Adam. 'It's his show.'

'Ah, the old man with the hair that looks ready to fly away like a great, grey bat?'

'That's him.'

'Can we get a *move* on, please?' snapped Angela, coming up behind the twins.

Lucian trembled visibly. 'Of course, madam.' And with that, he began painstakingly entering the names of the whole crew into the hotel register.

'This is going to take *forever*,' moaned Lana quietly.

'Come on,' said Adam, 'We've got the key. We can find our own way, whatever the Creepy Count says.'

Picking up his backpack, he dashed up the stairs. Lana sighed. It was just like Adam to go rushing off. Although she had to admit that the idea of finding a bed was very appealing . . .

She cast a glance back at the desk, but Angela was deeply engrossed in correcting Lucian's spelling of her name. She'd never notice they were gone. Grabbing her own bag, Lana followed her twin.

4

The stairs opened on to a broad landing that led into a long, wood-panelled corridor. Suits of armour stood guard and more oil paintings observed their progress.

One portrait, bigger than all the others, dominated the corridor. It showed a hard-faced man dressed in old-fashioned clothing, standing in front of Castle Dragomir. His lips were thin and cruel, set in an imperious sneer. But even more chilling was the enormous, savage-looking beast that crouched at his feet, its bared fangs and fierce, glaring eyes making it look as if it was about to devour the painter.

'Beware of the dog,' murmured Adam.

'Looks more like a dog crossed with a wolf,' replied Lana with a shiver, remembering the terrifying chase through the forest.

Adam studied the inscription on the heavy gold frame: *Count Ladislau Dragomir (1867–1930)*. 'One of the Count's ancestors,' he mused. 'Freaky looks must run in the family.'

'Whoever it is, he's long dead, so can we just find our room, please?'

Adam grinned and opened his eyes wide. 'Long dead maybe, but perhaps his ghost still haunts these halls . . .'

Lana gave her brother a playful shove. 'Stop it. Now, let's get going.' She studied the walls, but there were no helpful signs to direct them to Room 124. In fact, in the dim light it was barely possible to make out the numbers of the rooms at all. The corridor was filled with shadowy doorways and darkened windows. Lana shivered again. Perhaps they should have waited for Lucian after all.

'Come on!' called Adam. 'It must be on this floor somewhere.' He ducked down through a low archway and into an even darker passageway. The floor was crooked and uneven, and the floorboards creaked alarmingly.

'Um, Adam, I'm not sure this is the right way.'

'Well, let's just get to the end and –'

Knock-knock-knock!

A hollow sound echoed down the passage.

'What was that?' Adam looked over his shoulder.

'Dunno,' replied his sister. 'Dodgy pipes?'

Knock-knock-knock!

The sound echoed again, closer this time.

'It doesn't sound much like pipes.'

Knock-knock-knock!

This time, the noise was right above their heads. Lana felt a light scattering of dust settle on her hair.

'Could be a poltergeist,' said Adam excitedly. 'Oh wow!'

Knock-knock-knock!

This time Lana felt the floor beneath her vibrate, almost as if the wooden boards were trying to shake her off her feet. The corridor seemed to have become colder, and a chilly draught was dancing across her skin. It was like someone – or some*thing* – didn't want them there.

Knock-knock-knock!

Now the sound was right next to the twins, like a fist pounding on the wall, trying to break through and grab hold of them.

'Come on, Adam, let's go.' Lana walked on faster, trying not to imagine what could be causing the strange noise.

Knock-knock-knock!

The sound came again, even louder. Lana saw the dusty floorboards shake as an invisible force rapped against them.

Gritting her teeth to hold in a squeal of fright, Lana broke into a run. There was a doorway just ahead. Light gleamed welcomingly, but her brother was still gazing at the floor. 'Come *on*, Adam!'

Suddenly, she was out of the corridor, standing on a warmly-lit landing, Adam reluctantly emerging after her. As his feet left the rickety planks of the corridor and touched the plush carpet of the landing, the knocking instantly vanished.

'That,' he proclaimed, 'was a seriously spooky experience.'

Lana pulled herself together – the late night must be really affecting her. 'OK, it was a bit strange, but there could be any number of sensible explanations. Maybe the boards were all loose, and us walking on them made them vibrate. You saw how it stopped the moment we left the corridor.'

'Yeah – or it could have been a ghost.'

Lana shook her head. Her brother always looked for the most implausible explanation.

'Where are we anyway?' he asked, scanning the doors that led off the landing. 'We should make a note of the location so that Uncle Larry can check it out.'

'I don't think we're going to have a problem finding it again,' replied Lana, nodding towards the large brass plaque on the nearest door.

Room 124

'Cool. Right next to the Haunted Corridor,' smirked Adam.

'Yeah. Great.'

'Well, let's get inside. Maybe we have our own ghost in the room too,' said Adam. Lana gasped. 'I wasn't serious, you know,' continued Adam, but his sister wasn't listening. She was staring straight ahead. 'What is it?'

Without a word, Lana just pointed at the large, brightly polished plate that showed their room number. It was so shiny that Adam could see his own face in it. And Lana's. And the other girl.

Other girl?

Slowly, the twins turned round. Behind them,

the Haunted Corridor yawned emptily. There was nobody there. And when they turned back, the third face had vanished from the reflection as if it had never existed.

5

Adam had lied.

Whatever he was doing on his laptop, it *was* keeping Lana awake. For the twentieth time, she tossed and turned pointedly. But her brother continued to ignore her.

Once they had got into their room, Lana had decided to go straight to bed. She had hoped that sleep might help her forget the reflected face that had vanished so strangely. It wasn't working. Not only was Adam's computer screen casting a faint glow up the wall but, however deep she buried her head in the pillow, Lana could still hear the irritating *tap-tap-tap* of the keyboard, reminding her uncomfortably of the *knock-knock-knock* in the corridor just outside their door . . .

Finally, she growled and sat up.

Adam glanced across from his bed, all innocence. 'Can't sleep?' He was deliberately trying to wind her up now.

'Oh, ha ha. What's so important that you couldn't wait and look it up in the morning?'

Adam looked at her for a moment, wondering if she was really interested. 'Our friend from the portrait, Ladislau Dragomir. Vampires. Wallachia.'

'Wallachia?'

'That's where we are. It's just south of Transylvania,' he added, lending significant weight to the last word.

'I know.' Lana stifled a yawn, then tried to rub some life into her eyes. 'But it's pronounced with a "v" – "Vall-a-chee-a".'

Adam grinned and for a moment Lana thought he was going to tease her, but instead he said, 'Thanks. See, that's what makes us such a good team.'

'What? You know about the ghosts and vampires and things like that, and I know about all the real stuff?'

'I'm not sure Fergus would like to be called

unreal.' Adam smiled. 'It's a shame he didn't come with us.'

Lana shuffled over to sit on the side of her bed. 'Oh yes. Then you could both've kept me up. Anyway, it's no use moaning about that. He'll be fine back at Uncle Larry's. I'm sure he's having the time of his life. Well, you know what I mean.'

'Yeah, you're probably right. He might have helped us talk to that ghost in the corridor, though.'

'We don't know that was a ghost,' argued Lana.

'What about the face, then?' replied Adam.

'That could have been a trick of the light,' said his sister.

Adam chuckled. 'You don't really believe that. We've found our first spook of the trip.'

'Maybe,' grimaced Lana. 'Anyway, let's see what *you've* found.' She moved across to Adam's bed to get a better view of his computer screen.

'There's quite a lot. You know how the Count said that the character we know as Dracula was based on a real guy – Vlad Dracula?' Lana nodded.

'Well, Dracula might as well have been based on Ladislau Dragomir. He was horrible enough. He used to have his servants whipped for no reason, and he was particularly cruel to Romany people. Remember how Benedikte said that there were hardly any left in this area any more? Well, this is why.'

Adam clicked on the screen and an illustration appeared. It showed a terrible scene – in a forest clearing, a Romany camp was being attacked by dozens of ferocious dogs. Men, women and children were desperately trying to defend themselves, but it was clear that they didn't have a chance. It was a fairly crude drawing, but Lana had more than enough imagination to get an idea of how horrible it must have been for the poor victims.

'It was known as the Rundek Massacre,' continued Adam, 'after the Romany clan that was attacked. Count Ladislau Dragomir hated the Romany people so much that he set his hounds on them. Only one little boy survived. The whole of the Rundek Clan was wiped out.'

Lana shuddered and pushed the image out of her head. 'That's got to be worse than anything a vampire could do.'

'Yeah.' Adam grimaced. 'It's enough to put you off your dinner.' Sitting back, he patted his stomach. 'Although, saying that . . . I'm starving.'

Lana nodded. 'Me too. I haven't seen anything about room service. Maybe we should go down and see if there's any chance of an early breakfast.'

The bedside clock showed 4.30 a.m., which wasn't encouraging. Even so, Adam set aside his laptop and hopped off the bed. 'Nothing ventured, nothing gained.'

Putting on their slippers, the twins cautiously opened the door and went out on to the landing. Directly ahead, the Haunted Corridor yawned like the gaping mouth of a huge black snake. Lana felt a little shiver run down her spine. The corridor was silent now, but if they set foot inside it, would that strange knocking start up again? Lana knew it was silly to be afraid of an empty corridor, but she couldn't quite bring herself to step into it.

Lana glanced at her brother and, to her surprise, he looked a little worried too. Their eyes met and Adam gave his sister a sheepish smile. Without a word, they headed in the other direction, looking for another way down.

Now that the idea of food had whetted her appetite, Lana was ravenous. She and Adam prowled the halls of Castle Dragomir like a couple of hungry predators. Although since their ideal prey was a bacon sandwich, they hoped it wouldn't require any actual stalking.

In fact, their stealthy movements had more to do with not wishing to bump into Angela. She would definitely want to mount some late-night ghost watches during their brief stay, but not on the first night. The producer was almost certainly fast asleep, not patrolling the corridors like a prison guard, but where Angela was concerned, it was always better to be safe than sorry.

In the dim light, the old portraits and suits of armour, the landings and passageways looked like ideal haunting grounds for all manner of ghosts. Occasionally, though, as if the night itself was trying to spur on their imaginations, the silence would give way to the wild, sorrowful howl of wolves from somewhere in the forest.

'What was that?'

'What was what?' sighed Lana. Adam had

started hearing things almost as soon as they had left their room.

'It sounded like a voice. Listen.'

For a moment, Lana couldn't hear anything. Then, just as she was about to tell Adam that he was imagining it, she caught a low noise, almost too quiet to be heard. She held her breath. The sound came again, slightly louder this time.

'Is that somebody crying?' she whispered.

'That's what I thought,' replied Adam. 'Remember what the Count said about the castle ghosts sobbing in the night?'

'I thought he was making it up,' breathed Lana.

'You would.'

'Where's it coming from?'

'Round that bend in the corridor, I think,' murmured Adam. 'Let's see if we can get closer.'

On tiptoes, the twins crept towards the muffled sound. Carefully avoiding creaky floorboards, they inched forward until they reached a sharp bend in the corridor. The gentle weeping got slightly louder as they approached. Whatever was making the noise, it was just round the corner.

Ready? mouthed Adam silently. Lana nodded.

One, two –

But before Adam could reach *three*, the crying stopped abruptly. Silence filled the castle. Cautiously, the twins peered round the corner. Nothing. The corridor was empty.

'Where did they go?' Adam looked completely bemused.

'Maybe there was nobody here – or maybe the sound was coming from further off.'

Adam shook his head.

'Well, whatever it was, it's gone,' said Lana finally. 'So why don't we see if we can find that early breakfast?'

The twins made it downstairs without seeing or hearing anything else, but the main hall, though well-lit, was silent and deserted.

Crossing the hall, the twins poked their heads into the dining room, but the bare tables lay shrouded in pristine white tablecloths, and the room was empty and dark, apart from an illuminated strip at the far end of the room where moonlight slanted in through tall French windows.

It looked like any leftovers had been safely tucked away in the kitchen. Back home, the twins could have just raided the fridge, but even the most relaxed and hospitable of hotels would frown on guests rummaging around the larder for midnight snacks.

'Oh, well,' said Lana, 'I guess we'll have to struggle through till breakfast. They'll probably serve it quite early.'

'Not early enough,' grumbled Adam, glancing out of the window.

Moonlight bathed the castle grounds. The lawn was frosted with silver and stars twinkled above the dark stables. Everything seemed peaceful and still. So Adam caught his breath sharply as a dark shape scythed through the night.

A bat. A big bat. And it wasn't alone. A second pair of fluttering wings swooped across the garden, heading for the stables. Then a third. And a fourth. Suddenly, the air was thick with them. Their wings seemed to blot out the moon as they sped over the garden and spiralled down into the stables.

Lana gripped her brother's arm. She'd always hated bats.

'Don't worry, Lana,' soothed Adam as the last of the creatures disappeared from view. 'They're gone now.'

But even as he spoke, Adam spotted more movement from the stables. As the twins watched, the door opened and a thin, shadowy figure emerged.

Locking the door behind him, the Count began walking briskly towards the French windows.

The *open* French windows.

Lana could have sworn they had been closed when she first came into the room. But they were wide open now and the Count was definitely heading towards them.

Soundlessly, the twins ducked under the nearest table, peering out from beneath the tablecloth. They held their breath as the Count entered, fastened the windows behind him and strode past their hiding place, his long legs so close that the twins could have reached out and touched them. For what seemed like an age, they stayed absolutely still. But there was no sound. Cautiously, the twins emerged.

'Did you see that?' whispered Adam. 'He must

have transformed into a bat and been off doing all sorts of evil things.'

'Don't be ridiculous, Adam. Just because we saw some bats doesn't mean the Count's a vampire.'

'We'll see,' replied Adam grimly. 'Come on. We'd better get back to bed before he catches us and sucks our blood.'

Tiptoeing across the main hall, the twins sneaked up the grand staircase and back to their room. Once they were safely back inside, Adam let out a long whistle.

'What did I tell you? Spooky things are definitely happening. There's something very, *very* strange going on in this castle.'

6

Morning arrived noisily and early.

Adam and Lana's restless dreams had been filled with the sounds of howling and crying echoing down empty hallways, but they woke to the roar of engines, the grinding of wheels on gravel and the low drone of some other huge engine. Throwing off his covers, Adam scrambled across Lana's bed to the window and yanked open the curtain to see what new kind of chaos had descended on the castle.

The sun was barely peeking over the mountains and the land lay in semi-darkness under a sky of blood-reds and fiery yellows. Suddenly, a helicopter came buzzing in, alarmingly low, and whizzed overhead in a dramatic blur.

Below it, a convoy of gleaming white Land Rovers was snaking through the castle gate and up the drive. As they raced for the best spaces in the car park, Adam and Lana could see that their roof racks were heavily laden with cases and equipment – and that every bonnet was marked with the same lurid logo: *Ghosts Unlimited*.

'What's going on?' asked Lana groggily. Blinking, she stumbled over to join Adam at the window. 'Oh no . . .'

Pyjamas and dressing gowns flapping in the powerful wind from the rotors, the *Fright Night* crew poured out through the front door, just behind Adam and Lana. The helicopter had circled around Castle Dragomir and was now hovering over the broad expanse of lawn.

Clutching his wig, Uncle Larry looked dismayed. 'Oh dear,' he moaned, surveying the scene unhappily. 'What on earth can *they* be doing here?'

Ghosts Unlimited was *Fright Night's* arch-rival TV programme – and was almost always ahead of them in the ratings war. Of course it helped that *Ghosts Unlimited* regularly used fake monsters and computer-generated ghosts to liven up their episodes.

'Don't worry, Uncle Larry,' snarled Adam, who hated the show more than anything in the world. 'Angela will send them packing.' Uncle Larry gave Adam a hopeful smile, but the *Ghosts Unlimited* crew were already spilling from the parked cars and unloading the roof racks.

Angela, meanwhile, looked like a nuclear reactor about to blow. She paced up and down in front of the stone steps, fists clenched, as though searching for someone to punch.

As the rotors wound to a stop, a figure jumped out of the helicopter and began to stride confidently towards the castle. Adam and Lana recognized him instantly.

Stuart Smythe.

Suave and handsome, his dark hair arranged a little too perfectly on his head, the *Ghosts Unlimited* presenter approached the castle with the manner of someone who, if he didn't already own the place, was at least considering buying it. His smile was big and broad, showing off a set of teeth that gleamed like they belonged in a toothpaste advert.

Uncle Larry mumbled miserably to himself. Lana gave him a sympathetic smile. It was bad enough to be pitted directly opposite your rival in the TV schedules, but much worse to have the competition show up at the same location. However, it didn't look like Angela was going down without a fight.

She stormed forward. '*What*,' she bellowed, with enough volume to be heard across several valleys, 'is the meaning of this?'

Smythe's dazzling smile didn't falter. 'Angela Clancy. Fancy meeting you here.' He held out his hand. Angela ignored it. 'This is a film crew. I imagine you must have seen one of those before.'

'Yes, thank you. And at this precise moment I'm seeing one too many around here. So I suggest your people pack up and turn themselves around, while you shove off in your fancy helicopter.'

'Sorry, Angie, no can do. We're booked in, fair and square.' Smythe spread his hands in mock apology. 'Didn't the Count mention we were coming?' he added innocently.

'Where is the Count?' murmured Adam pointedly. 'Nowhere to be seen, now that the sun's up!'

'He is the owner of the hotel, Adam. He probably lets his staff handle this kind of thing,'

Lana pointed out. She gave him a hard stare, to let him know she knew precisely what he was thinking. 'Just because he isn't around that doesn't mean he's up to no good.'

'I never said he was,' said Adam, although his mind was buzzing.

'Now, now, children,' Uncle Larry appealed. 'We need to hear what's going on.'

Angela was fuming. 'No, the Count did *not* tell me you were coming. But we are going to sit down and *talk*, Mr Smythe, and we are going to sort this out.'

'Fine. Let's talk.'

'Not until I've had some breakfast,' retorted Angela furiously. 'And got dressed.'

'Why?' asked Smythe smoothly, looking Angela up and down. 'I hear dressing gowns are what all the really fashionable TV professionals are wearing these days.'

Angela shot a venomous look at both the *Ghosts Unlimited* and *Fright Night* crews, immediately silencing anyone who had dared to chuckle. 'There'll be a meeting in one hour. In the dining room. Everyone – be there.'

With that, she marched back into the castle, brushing rather roughly past poor Uncle Larry.

Smythe followed, casting his beaming smile over everyone. He gave Uncle Larry a friendly nod. 'Larry Craddock, old man. Good to see you.' Then he was up the steps, through the doorway and inside the castle, leaving Uncle Larry looking like somebody who had been washed ashore after a shipwreck.

'Yes, well, and – of course – good to see you too,' he stammered helplessly, before hurrying inside. Adam and Lana felt bad for him. As the rest of the *Fright Night* and *Ghosts Unlimited* crews filed slowly past, they eyed each other warily.

'This could mean trouble,' muttered Lana.

Adam rolled his eyes. 'You don't say! If we give him half a chance, old Slimy Smythe will steal our stories.'

'What stories?'

'The Haunted Corridor and the Vampire Count of course!' replied Adam.

'Adam –'

'I don't care what you say, I don't trust the Count,' interrupted Adam, staring towards the stables where they had last seen him. 'And I want to know what he was doing out there in the middle of the night. I'm going to take a look.' Stifling a yawn, Lana followed her brother.

The stables looked old and ramshackle, with sagging walls and damp woodwork, but they were surprisingly secure. Apart from a couple of broken windows set high up in one wall (which looked like they might have been the entrance used by the bats the night before), the only way into the building was through a large set of doors – which were securely fastened with a hefty padlock. There was a fair-sized gap between the doors, though, and Adam went straight to it and pressed his face to the wood.

'All right,' said Lana. 'So what can you see?' She nervously glanced left and right, but there was no one nearby. Somehow, spying – even on a probably empty building – seemed like the wrong thing to be doing.

'Nothing. It's too dark.'

'Here, let me have a look,' snapped Lana impatiently. Ducking under her brother, she put her own eye to the gap and peered inside.

Even though the sun had now fully risen, it was still gloomy in the stable, and Lana had to wait while her eyes adjusted. At first, all she could see were grey, bulky objects in shadow, but slowly the shadows evolved into shapes: here, a set of wooden steps; there, a spoked wagon wheel, curved roofs and decorative trim. Even in the relative darkness, the twins could also see hints of bright colours, but it looked like paintwork that had faded or peeled.

'Caravans.'

'Yeah,' agreed Adam. 'Old ones. They look like they were made by Romany people.'

'But I thought the Count's ancestors hated them,' remarked Lana, puzzled. 'So why would he have their caravans?'

Just then a shadow fell across them. 'What are you doing here?' barked a voice.

The twins spun around – and found a tall, burly figure looming over them.

7

For a moment, the man glared at them fiercely. Then his bushy moustache twitched and he broke into a familiar raucous laugh.

'That gave you a shock, eh?' he chuckled. 'You look like you saw a ghost!'

'That was mean,' complained Lana. 'You gave us a real fright.'

But Adam was already grinning. 'Hello, Benedikte. What are you up to? Is this where you keep the carriage?'

'Ah no,' replied the coachman. 'There is another stable on the other side of the castle. This one is not used so much. Only by the Count.'

'Do you know what he does in there?' asked Adam quickly.

Benedikte smiled. 'Oh yes.'

'What?' enquired Lana, intrigued despite herself.

Benedikte regarded the twins, amused. 'Ah, but if I told you, what would be left for you to poke your noses into? Eh?' He sniffed dismissively. 'Besides, I think you would be *scared*.'

'Try us.'

'Adam,' cautioned Lana. After their experiences of the last twenty-four hours, she had no desire to be scared again.

'Is he a vampire?' asked Adam, undeterred.

'Vampire?' Benedikte raised his eyebrows. 'Ah, you are too young to know of such terrible things.'

'Uncle Larry says that you're never too young to learn about the supernatural. That's why he likes having me and Lana on the show. He says we're learning stuff that could save our lives.'

'Or put you in danger,' retorted Benedikte.

'You can at least tell us about the caravans in there,' wheedled Adam. 'They're Romany caravans, aren't they? What's the Count doing with them?'

Benedikte's face fell. 'The Count is a strange man – perhaps a dangerous man. There is nothing he will not exploit. I do not think that children are safe under his roof. You must take care.'

Adam pressed on. 'The Count's ancestors hated Romany people, though. One of them massacred the Rundek Clan, didn't he?'

Benedikte shot Adam a troubled glance. 'What do you know of the massacre?' he demanded.

'We read about it last night,' said Lana.

'Yeah,' Adam beamed. 'There's loads of information online.'

Benedikte's worried frown only deepened at Adam's words. He crouched down, bringing his eyes level with the twins'.

'Listen – if you really want to uncover the secrets of this place, I can help you. But you will have to trust me.'

'All right,' said Adam. 'What can you tell us?'

'Not tell you – show you. There is something in the forest that you should see.'

'OK. Let's go.' Lana bit her lip. Why did her brother have to be so headstrong?

'Not now,' said Benedikte, standing up. 'Later. Today, I must work. Tonight, I will show you the path – for the woods hide many dangers and it is easy to lose your way.'

Lana shuddered. The thought of being lost in the depths of a dark Romanian forest was quite terrifying. Almost as if he was reading her thoughts, Benedikte smiled comfortingly. 'Do not fear. If you wish to learn about the Count, meet me at the gate at dusk. I will be your guide. But listen – do not mention the Rundek Massacre to anyone. It is a dangerous subject.' Benedikte nodded meaningfully towards the castle. 'Some people wish the past to remain hidden – and will do anything to keep it that way.' With a bow, he put on his hat and strode away.

'See,' crowed Adam. 'He doesn't trust the Count either.'

'Maybe,' said Lana. 'But if Benedikte dislikes the Count so much, why does he work for him?'

'He's probably got no choice. There can't be many jobs around here.'

'Maybe not. But . . .' Lana's voice dropped away. 'Look over there, Adam,' she hissed, pointing through a small gateway that led into the forest.

Just beyond the gate crouched a boy. He didn't look much older than the twins – a couple of years at the most – and was dressed in a weatherbeaten sheepskin jacket and baggy cloth cap. He was staring at the ground, almost as if he was trying to read it like a book, but as Adam took a step towards him, the boy jumped to his feet and raised his fists.

Adam froze, but Lana smiled encouragingly. 'Hello,' she said. 'I'm Lana.'

The boy pursed his lips warily. 'Hello,' he said. His accent was even stronger than Benedikte's. 'I am Nicolai.'

'Pleased to meet you, Nicolai,' Lana continued. 'This is Adam, my brother. We're staying at the castle. What are you doing?'

'I am hunting,' said Nicolai harshly. 'Have you seen the Beast?'

'The Beast?' Adam replied. 'What Beast?'

'The *varcolac*. It has killed my sheep.'

'*Varcolac?*' exclaimed Adam sharply.

'What's that?' asked Lana, surprised by her brother's reaction.

Adam took a deep breath. 'It's the Romanian word for werewolf.'

8

'Werewolf?' scoffed Lana.

'Yes, werewolf,' snapped Adam impatiently. 'You know, a human who turns into a wolf when there's a full moon.'

'It's probably just a local superstition about a normal wolf. There are enough of them about.'

'No!' Nicolai shook his head violently. 'There *is* a werewolf. You have seen it?'

Adam grimaced with disappointment. 'Sorry, mate. We haven't. Nobody's even mentioned a *varcolac.*'

Nicolai looked crestfallen. 'It is here − in this forest. I have tracked it. Soon I will find it. And then . . .' The shepherd boy dug into one of the many pockets of his jacket and produced a small hide pouch. Tipping the contents into his hand, he let them roll around in his palm, gleaming and jingling. They looked like small metal marbles.

Lana raised a quizzical eyebrow. 'What are they?'

'Silver bullets.'

'Whoa,' said Adam. 'You know your stuff. Silver is the only way to kill a werewolf,' he explained, seeing Lana's blank expression. 'Nothing else can harm them. Legend says that they are incredibly strong and tough, and that they heal really fast from even the most serious wounds.'

'And like most legends, I don't suppose these actually contain any real proof, do they?' asked Lana sarcastically.

'Laugh all you like,' replied her brother. 'There are accounts of werewolves throughout history – particularly from this part of eastern Europe. And silver bullets are the best way to kill them. But those aren't like any bullets I've ever seen.'

'They are for my catapult,' replied Nicolai.

'You're not seriously going to hunt a *wolf* with a *catapult*?' said Lana incredulously.

Nicolai didn't reply. He simply picked up a small stone from the ground, loaded it into his catapult, took aim at a nearby tree and fired. With a loud splintering of wood, the stone slammed into a branch, splitting it in two.

Adam and Lana gasped. Nicolai smirked. 'It is a good catapult.'

'Too right!' agreed Adam. 'Well, good luck, Nicolai. If we see anything, we'll let you know.'

Nicolai grinned toothily. 'Thank you. I go now.' And with that, he slipped away through the trees, as silent as a wolf himself.

'Ghosts, vampires *and* werewolves?' Lana threw up her hands. 'This is getting ridiculous.'

'Just imagine if we did find a werewolf, though,' replied Adam, eyes gleaming. 'That would make a pretty good episode of *Fright Night*.'

Lana frowned. 'If *Ghosts Unlimited* don't find it first. Speaking of which, we'd better get back. If we miss the meeting, Angela will go ballistic.'

*

With a bossy *clink* of her spoon against her teacup, Angela called the meeting to order.

Both the *Fright Night* and *Ghosts Unlimited* crews had eaten ces that weren't glum belonged to Angela, who was still seething, and Stuart Smythe, who leaned back in his chair with the smug grin of a man who hadn't a care in the world.

'The way I see it,' began Angela, 'it's simple. Owing to some apparent *oversight* on the Count's part, we have one too many television crews here at the castle. But *Fright Night* was here first. I'm sure that *Ghosts Unlimited* will be able to make an exit just as grand as this morning's showy entrance.' She laid her teaspoon on her saucer and sat down.

Smythe flashed his brilliant smile. 'I realize our arrival may have had a few of you jumping out of the wrong side of bed. But it was a perfect opportunity to get some shots from the air. Nothing quite like an aerial long shot to open an episode, is there, Angie?'

Angela ground her teeth. Of course, Smythe knew full well that *Fright Night* could never afford aerial shots. 'Take my word for it,' he added smugly, 'this place looks spectacular from the air.'

Smythe's grin widened. He was clearly taking great pleasure in the sight of Angela seething. Normally, Adam and Lana might have found that amusing too, but this man was making fun of Uncle Larry's show – and that got the twins just as mad as Angela.

'Anyway, Angie,' continued Smythe, 'let's face facts. I have as much right to make my show here as you have to film one of your dreary, ghost-free documentaries.'

'Now, I really must object –' began Uncle Larry.

'Oh, do be quiet,' interrupted Angela. 'Don't rise to his bait.' She drew a deep breath, obviously finding it hard to follow her own advice. 'The only fact we need to face is that, as grand as this old castle is, it's *not* big enough for two TV crews. I won't stand for your people getting in the way.'

'Ditto,' said Smythe flatly, as though that solved everything.

'Perhaps I may be of some assistance,' said a voice from the doorway.

Everyone turned to see the Count making a

modest entrance, one hand smoothing his dark suit. 'I heard there was some dispute.'

Lana leaned closer to her brother and out of the side of her mouth said, 'Look – the Count's walking about in the daytime without bursting into flames.' She was no vampire expert, but she knew enough to tell that this was proof that Adam's suspicions were wrong.

'OK, so maybe he's not a vampire,' admitted Adam with a disappointed frown, 'but that doesn't mean he's not up to no good.' And with that, he pulled out his mobile phone and began moodily stabbing buttons. Lana sighed. The last thing she needed now was for Adam to go into one of his sulks.

'Come on,' Lana whispered, pulling the phone out of his hand and putting it on the table. 'We need to pay attention to what's going on.'

'I'm afraid,' said Angela, standing up, her voice dangerously calm, 'there appears to have been some sort of *mistake*. Another TV crew has arrived this morning. They say *you* invited them.'

'Ah, my humblest apologies.' The Count shook his head regretfully. 'I had not realized it would create such problems. I am very proud of the castle, and I wanted all the world to know about the ghosts that haunt these ancient halls. So I made my invitation to two television programmes. I realize now, of course, I should have consulted each of you more closely. I am sorry.' He gave a low bow.

'Yes, that's all very well,' snapped Angela, 'but we can't *both* do a show on the castle ghosts. It's absurd. There might not be enough to go round!'

'What about the werewolf?'

'Adam!' hissed Lana. 'What are you doing?'

'Werewolf?' The Count looked confused.

'Yeah,' continued Adam. 'We just met a boy who says there's a werewolf in the forest.'

'I have never heard of such a creature,' exclaimed the Count.

'Werewolf, you say?' Stuart Smythe's ears had pricked up at the first mention of the word.

'A *werewolf*?' boomed Angela, ignoring Smythe completely. 'What nonsense!'

'It's not nonsense. Nicolai is hunting it. He had silver bullets and everything. It could be a great story. If we –'

'Ghosts!' interrupted Uncle Larry abruptly,

banging his hand down on the table and almost sending the marmalade flying. 'Um, sorry, Adam,' he said, eyes flitting nervously around the room. 'All I mean to say is, ah, well, the ghosts. Those are what I came for really.' He appealed to Angela. 'So, um, if Smythe is so interested in the werewolf, why don't we just let him have the story? We can concentrate on the ghosts.'

'That's actually not a bad suggestion, Larry,' remarked Angela.

Smythe considered for a moment, then nodded decisively. 'It makes sense. We're the bigger outfit, so we get the bigger story.'

'It's agreed, then?' snapped Angela.

'Absolutely. It's agreed.'

Adam couldn't believe it. Smythe was acting like he was doing *Fright Night* a favour, when in fact he'd just muscled in and pinched the best story the programme had ever found. But before he could speak, Angela took charge.

'Very well. This is how it's going to work,' she announced to the entire room. '*Ghosts Unlimited* will be covering the werewolf story. *Fright Night* will be exploring the castle ghosts. And the two sides will stay as far apart as possible.'

Adam could contain himself no longer. 'What if we discover something about the werewolf? We had loads of ghosts in the last episode. Won't the viewers want something different?'

'That's quite enough, young man,' barked Angela. 'I think I know better than you what our viewers want.'

'Now, now, Angie,' slimed Smythe. 'The lad has a point. How about we make a deal? Both crews will keep their eyes open for ghosts *and* werewolves. If you guys get any good werewolf footage, you give it to us. And naturally we'll hand over any film of ghosts to you.'

'Done!' agreed Angela.

'Yeah, because that's fair!' shouted Adam, jumping to his feet and pointing accusingly at Stuart Smythe. 'You never get any film of ghosts because you put them all in with computers afterwards. You're a fraud!'

'Are you suggesting that our spooks are in some way *manufactured*? I'm shocked and offended at the accusation.'

Smythe didn't look it, though. Instead, he shared a laugh with the weaselly-looking *Ghosts Unlimited* cameraman next to him. Adam felt like pushing Smythe's fake-tanned face into what was left of his full English breakfast. It was people like him that gave paranormal investigation a bad name.

'Don't be rude, Adam,' said Uncle Larry with a frown. 'We may not approve of Mr Smythe's methods, but there's no need to shout.' Scowling, Adam sat down.

'Right,' said Angela, 'I will take the camera crew into town this morning to film some footage to establish the *setting*. Then it's an all-night ghost watch tonight.' The *Fright Night* crew groaned.

'Save your complaints. I want to see you all at the gate in half an hour. Not you, Adam and Lana. We can do without you cluttering up the set. That will be all.'

At the next table, Smythe stretched lazily. 'I think I'll have a quick game of tennis. And then perhaps a sauna.' He waved an airy hand in the direction of the *Ghosts Unlimited* crew. 'Why don't you all take the morning off? We'll start filming later.'

Chattering and laughing, Smythe's cronies drifted off, smirking at the *Fright Night* crew, who muttered rebelliously and shot dirty looks at Angela. Only Uncle Larry seemed happy.

Adam seethed inwardly. One thing was crystal clear: Stuart Smythe was trouble.

Big trouble.

9

'I can't believe Angela just gave up on the werewolf story,' complained Adam as he and Lana slipped out of the dining room. 'I bet it's just cos she's scared of wolves.'

'Could be,' agreed his sister. 'But we don't even know for sure that there *is* a werewolf. Smythe might end up running around the forest on a wild goose chase.'

'True,' replied Adam, 'but Nicolai seemed very certain, didn't he?'

'Yeah,' Lana admitted. 'But anyway, we can always find out more about the werewolf ourselves.'

'Yeah. And we also need to uncover what the Count was up to last night.'

'OK,' said Lana, 'let's wait for him to come out.' She had barely spoken when the tall figure of

Count Dragomir emerged from the dining room. Adam leaped in front of him. 'Hello,' he said.

'Good morning, children.' The Count put on a smile the same way some people put on a tie. 'Is everything all right?'

Adam beamed innocently. 'We were just wondering what was in the stables? Over there?' He pointed out through the French windows.

Lana grimaced. Her brother wasn't being nearly as subtle as he thought he was, but the Count seemed unfazed, conjuring another smile with the faintest of efforts.

'Nothing very much. Antique Romany caravans.'

'Sounds cool. Can we see them?'

The Count's smile wavered. 'I am afraid not. They are all very old and in poor repair. It could be dangerous for children.'

'If they're in such a bad state, why are you keeping them?'

The Count's smile was more like a grimace now. 'I have always been fascinated by the history of the Romany people. I have plans to turn one floor of the castle into a museum of Romany culture. I inherited the caravans from my grandfather, Ladislau . . .'

Adam's eyebrows flew up so fast they almost hit the ceiling. So the infamous Ladislau Dragomir was the Count's *grandfather*. He shot his twin a significant look as the Count continued speaking.

'One day, I hope to restore them. Once they are returned to their former glory, they will be the centrepiece of my exhibition. Now −' he made another of his curt bows − 'I must go.' And with that, the Count marched off.

'That man is definitely hiding something.'

'You may be right.' Lana didn't like jumping to conclusions, but at the same time she didn't like what her instincts were telling her. She'd been proved right in her belief that the Count was not a vampire, but there *was* something about him that bothered her. 'Maybe he's got a guilty conscience. His grandfather was really horrible to the Romany people. Maybe this is his way of saying sorry.'

Her brother snorted, but Lana pressed on anyway. 'Besides, why would a man who has something to hide invite *two* television crews into his home?'

Adam opened his mouth to reply, but he had no answer to that. 'OK, that's a good point,' he said eventually. 'I bet he does have some sort of secret reason, though. He's clearly dodgy. We really need to find out more about him. We've got to go to the forest with Benedikte and find out what he's got to tell us – or show us.'

Lana sighed. She should have seen that coming.

Several hours later, the twins were back in the horse-drawn carriage, rattling and bumping into the darkness and the unknown. Lana was nervous, but she did her best to hide it. The forbidding pine trees flashed quickly past, reminding her of their first madcap journey to the castle when the wolves had chased the carriage. The sun had already sunk beneath the rim of the mountains, and the world was fading into grey and black shadow.

Despite her misgivings, Lana hadn't put up much of a fight against Adam's suggestion of going with Benedikte. Her brother was determined, and that was that. So she had decided to hide her reservations and play along for his sake – and to make sure they were back at the castle in time for the night's filming.

There was a lot of preparation involved in staging a ghost watch, and Angela never liked the twins hanging around while the crew were getting everything set up. So she and Uncle Larry had readily agreed that Adam and Lana could amuse themselves until eight o'clock.

That gave them two hours, and Adam had promised that they wouldn't need more than that to get to the forest and back. Not for the first time, Lana had to place her trust in her brother's confidence that everything would be all right. Not for the first time, she wondered if they weren't making a really bad decision.

But the rules were different for Lana and Adam, weren't they? They were part of a TV crew, investigating the supernatural; they had to take a few risks to uncover the truth. It was what they had done in Ireland, chasing off after a witch with a ghost in tow.

Lana had definitely learned one lesson on that trip, though – that they should never go off on their own without making sure that *somebody* knew where they were going. Adam wouldn't agree of course, but what he didn't know couldn't hurt him . . .

The twins gripped the edge of their seats tightly as the speeding carriage rounded another tight hairpin bend. Benedikte glanced back at them often, as if he was afraid they might somehow vanish. He had taken good care of them so far, although Lana wished he didn't have to drive *quite* so fast.

Lana caught his eye and Benedikte cracked a broad smile and let out another of his warm, throaty chuckles. 'Relax. I know these roads like my own brothers and sisters.'

'Are you from a big family, Benedikte?' asked Lana as she watched the trees rushing past in the gathering dark.

'Yes, a very big family,' replied the coachman. 'Big family here in the forest. You will meet them soon.' He cracked the whip again and the horses picked up even more speed.

Adam, who had been quiet for a while, said, 'We know it's true that there are caravans in that stable – we've seen them ourselves – but the Count could have *anything* hidden inside them.'

'That's true,' admitted Lana, not really wanting to hear more of Adam's speculations.

'Wait, wait,' Benedikte advised, turning to look at them over his shoulder. 'Soon you will know the secret.'

Suddenly, the carriage lurched violently. Benedikte snapped his head round to the front and tried to slow the horses, but it was too late. Neighing with fear, the horses veered one way; the carriage swung the other. Benedikte tugged on the reins again, but they were going too fast to stop. The wheels must have overshot the roadside because suddenly the carriage was toppling . . .

Clutching on to his sister, Adam heard the loud crack of something snapping and realized it must have been the harness, because he could still hear the horses' hooves galloping away as the carriage thumped and bumped down a steep embankment, trees coming at them from every direction. Then there was a huge crunch and, with a vicious splintering of wood, everything seemed to come to a juddering halt.

Except Lana and Adam. They carried on – thrown through the air – until they hit the ground hard, the breath smacked out of them. Everything fell still and deathly quiet.

Somewhere in the forest, wolves howled.

10

At the sound of the wolves, Lana struggled to her feet — and then wished she hadn't. She hurt all over. Luckily, nothing seemed broken, but she could tell that she would be covered in bruises tomorrow. Adam looked pale and dazed but otherwise unharmed. He squeezed his sister's hand.

'Are you OK?'

'I'll live,' Lana nodded. 'But what about Benedikte?'

Adam knelt forward, then crawled to the overturned carriage, where they could only see the top half of their driver sticking out from underneath the battered vehicle.

'I am hurt,' groaned Benedikte as they approached, his voice croaking with pain. 'I can't move. My leg — it is crushed, broken. I can feel it.'

'OK. Don't panic.' Adam dug in his jacket pocket for his mobile phone. But the screen barely had a chance to light up before his face fell.

'Don't tell me,' said Lana, reading his expression. 'No signal.' A look at her own phone confirmed it. 'Why is it that whenever we're in trouble, there's no signal?'

Picking a point a short way from where Benedikte was pinned, Adam slid his hands under the carriage and gave an experimental heave. He might as well have been trying to lift Castle Dragomir.

'There's no way we're going to be able to get that off him ourselves. And we can't just sit here hoping that someone will pass by − he's badly hurt. Maybe if we climb up to the road, we can follow it back to the castle and . . . oh no.'

'What is it?'

Without another word, Adam pointed to the top of the slope down which they had crashed. Barely visible through the gathering darkness, Lana could just make out a group of dark shapes nosing over the ridge, sniffing the chill night air. She didn't need a closer look to know what they must be.

'Wolves,' Adam whispered.

'Listen,' rasped Benedikte, as though every word involved an incredible effort. 'I am trapped. You must go! Get away! Now!'

'We can't leave you!' hissed Adam fiercely. 'What about the wolves?'

'Listen, Adam,' replied Lana, 'if we find some higher ground, we might get a signal and call for help. But we've got to go *now*!'

'Yes,' said Benedikte. 'You must go!'

Reluctantly, Adam agreed. Crouching low, the twins scrambled towards a narrow path leading deeper into the forest. As she looked back, Lana saw the first wolf starting down the slope.

Turning away, Lana and Adam plunged into the trees.

They were lost. It was frightening how quickly the forest and the wolves had made sure of that.

The path that they had taken was overgrown, and the trees seemed to close ranks to conceal the way ahead. The cloudy night blotted out the moon and allowed little light to filter down to the forest floor. The twins had only been running for what seemed like a few minutes when they realized that the path had disappeared altogether. Now they were blindly pressing on, straining their eyes to catch a gleam of light in the darkness.

Breaking into a small clearing, the twins paused to catch their breath and assess their choices.

'In theory,' said Adam, pointing to the left, 'we should just keep going uphill. That way, we'll eventually make it back to the castle.'

Lana wasn't so sure. 'I don't know, Adam. There are an awful lot of uphills around here. We could be climbing the wrong side of the valley for all we know.' She examined her mobile phone. Still no signal. 'Well, we might as well try it,' she said and set off up the slope. Far above their heads, an owl hooted mournfully as if disapproving of their choice.

The path was steep, and the darkness and the thick undergrowth made it tough going, but for now at least it seemed like they'd lost the wolves. The shadows between the trees were just shadows.

'Look!' called Adam suddenly. He was only a metre or so in front of his sister and Lana's eyes quickly spotted what had caught his attention.

Light. Pale and watery, as though reflected up from a rippling pool. It bathed the surrounding trees, and shadows danced at its edges.

'It's the campfire we saw last night!' declared Adam. 'Maybe it's those local kids Benedikte mentioned. Come on!' He started forward eagerly.

'Adam, wait!' said Lana. 'There's something funny . . .' But Adam was already running down the slope towards the glow. Calling her brother a rude name under her breath, Lana followed.

As she threaded through the trees, trying to catch up with him, Lana glanced down at the light. Within the brightness, figures moved – white shadows in the light, growing steadily clearer as the twins came closer. Men and women danced in the warm light of a campfire.

'Hey! Over here!' called Adam. 'Hey! We need help!'

'Adam!' Lana hissed another warning. But it was no use. Even if he was still in earshot, her brother wasn't listening.

And there was definitely something strange about the camp. The figures dancing were certainly human, but somehow insubstantial, like luminous mist. Lana thought she could hear the sorrowful strains of a violin, but the music was as thin and frail as the lace-like figures.

Suddenly, Lana's foot thumped into something solid and woody. She went tumbling forward, over and over through a tangle of undergrowth, crashing into Adam and knocking them both down the slope and out into the middle of a clearing.

All around them stood Romany people. But the tall figures were all dressed in old-fashioned clothing − long, flowing skirts, baggy trousers and billowing shirts − like something out of a history book. And then Lana noticed something else about them.

Every single one was a ghost.

Just like the spirits the twins had seen in Ireland, these ghosts seemed to have been painted on to thin air. Their glowing white bodies were see-through, and floated just above the ground. But the twins could see the spectres looking directly at them, could feel their gaze like a chill breeze. Adam swallowed hard. There was no way of telling whether these ghosts would be friendly or not. He and Lana were all alone and entirely at their mercy . . .

For a long moment, there was silence. Then

one of the ghosts, a dark-eyed young girl with long, wispy hair, took a step towards them. With a shock, Lana recognized her – it was the girl whose face the twins had seen reflected in the brass plaque on their door in the hotel. She *had* been a ghost after all!

The spectral girl opened her mouth to speak, but at that very moment, she looked up sharply, as if she could hear something. Suddenly, Adam's vision swam. The white light of the camp blazed even brighter and, as he watched, one of the ghosts sailed into the air.

Whooshing straight past the twins, he disappeared between the trees, leaving only an icy wind in his wake. Then another of the ghosts came shooting by. Then more and more. The ghosts were being torn away from the camp, one by one, as though they were being tugged away by an invisible wire. The faint whine of violin strings became an anguished howl.

Adam hugged his sister, trembling as another ghost flashed through the air, terrifyingly close. The ghost passed just centimetres in front of them, its face twisted as if in pain. Adam winced at the sight.

The figures were gone in a matter of seconds. Last to leave was the girl, and as her ghostly form rushed past, a brilliant white streak on the air, Lana thought she heard a sorrowful cry that seemed strangely familiar.

As the twins watched, the phantom campfire died away to nothing. All that was left was darkness and a still, breathless silence. The twins lay there shivering, afraid to break the spell.

'Wow!' Adam breathed finally. 'How amazing was that?' He laughed shakily. 'Ghosts! A whole bunch of them!' He pulled out his mobile phone and waggled it in frustration. 'Should've taken pictures!'

'You couldn't have; they were way too fast.'

'True.' Adam snapped his fingers. 'Maybe they're the ghosts of the victims of the Rundek Massacre. It might have happened here, in this clearing – Fergus told us that some ghosts haunt the place where they once lived.'

Lana shook her head. 'But Romany people are travellers – they don't live in just one place, so wouldn't they travel around as ghosts, just like they did when they were alive?'

'Uncle Larry will know,' said Adam confidently.

'Perhaps he should be filming here in the forest instead of up at the castle.'

'But we've seen that girl in the castle too,' Lana reminded him. 'And did you hear her cry out just now? Her voice sounded just like that person we heard sobbing last night.'

Adam slapped his forehead and grinned. 'Of course! That's how we find our way back!'

'What are you talking about?' asked Lana, confused.

'Well, you're right – the first time we saw that girl ghost, she was in the castle. So I bet that's where they've all gone now! If we follow the ghosts, they'll lead us right there.'

'Come on, then,' said Lana excitedly, turning to go, but her brother grabbed her sleeve.

'Not that way.'

'Why not?'

'Because the wolves are back,' whispered Adam, pointing towards the grey shapes loping through the trees towards them.

The twins looked around frantically, but there was nowhere to run and it was too late to hide. The wolves had them surrounded.

But that wasn't the most terrifying thing. There was something strange about these silent creatures. Even from a distance, their eyes seemed to shine ghoulishly in the night. With a gulp, Adam and Lana remembered what Nicolai was supposed to be hunting. Was it possible that these were no ordinary wolves, but werewolves?

And as Adam and Lana watched the pack emerge from the trees, they could see without any doubt that the creatures' eyes were glowing with an unnatural green light.

With a snarl, the wolves closed in.

11

Backing up against the trunk of a nearby tree, Adam searched frantically around for something to use as a weapon, but the only thing he could find was a rotten branch.

Suddenly, under the wolves' low, hungry growling another sound emerged. A throaty roar that grew and grew as if another monster was invading the forest – from above.

Blinding light lanced down through the trees, fixing the twins and the wolf pack in its harsh glare. The air was whipped into a storm that set the branches above their heads thrashing violently. Leaves and twigs leaped off the forest floor and whirled about, while the swirling wind beat down on them like a tornado.

Shading their eyes against the dazzling light, the twins looked up. Above, they could just make out the shape of a helicopter hovering over the treetops. The largest wolf also turned his head and glared into the sky.

At the same moment, a gleaming silver streak shot through the air and slammed into the ground just in front of the lead wolf. Startled, the pack turned and bolted for the shadows.

Instantly, the spotlight swung away from the twins, chasing the pack across the clearing. A second silver streak flashed through the night. One of the pack jerked, flopped limply over, twitched once, then lay still.

Cautiously, Adam and Lana edged out from under their tree. With the blinding light and the churning air, they had to squint in order to see anything – and protect themselves from getting a stray twig in the eye. The searchlight danced unsteadily over the wolf's body as the helicopter hovered in the night sky, struggling to keep its bright eye on the kill.

Suddenly, a figure emerged from the trees behind Adam and Lana, clutching a catapult in one hand and wearing a familiar sheepskin jacket and tattered cap. Nicolai.

The shepherd boy turned to face the helicopter,

shouting loudly and waving his arms. Lana didn't speak Romanian but, judging by the gestures Nicolai was making, she suspected that most of the words he was using were very rude. Then he hurried over towards the twins.

'That,' said Adam, 'is what I call perfect timing! Thanks, Nicolai.'

Nicolai's eyes were dark and anxious. 'You are not harmed?' he asked. 'The wolves – they did not hurt you?'

'No,' replied Lana. 'Thanks to you.'

'But what are you doing? Why are you in forest?'

Lana glanced at her brother. 'We're looking for help. There was a crash. Benedikte – the man who drove us here in the carriage – he was hurt.'

Nicolai nodded. 'I saw carriage. Big wreck. All smashed up. But no one there.'

Adam and Lana frowned at each other. 'But Benedikte was pinned under the carriage,' said Adam. 'We had to leave him to get away from the wolves.'

Nicolai shook his head. 'He is not there now.'

Adam pursed his lips thoughtfully. 'That's very strange. Where did he go, then?'

'You saved our lives,' said Lana, trying to change the subject. 'Thanks. I was wrong about your catapult being no use against wolves – that was a great shot!'

Nicolai frowned angrily. 'No. Not great. Two shots. First shot missed. Not great.'

Adam patted him on the shoulder. 'It scared off the wolves, though. That was good enough for me!'

The helicopter was slowly descending now, coming in to land on the far side of the clearing. Unsurprisingly, the twins could see the *Ghosts Unlimited* logo on the side.

'Quick,' said Adam, 'let's get a look at the body before Smythe gets there.' And with that, he led the others hastily across the clearing. He took out his mobile and started filming.

The wolf lay sprawled untidily at the foot of a gnarled old tree. Its tongue lolled out between its fangs and the great head rested limply on the ground. The beast was deathly still. Nicolai spat a horrible-sounding Romanian curse.

'Looks dead all right,' said Lana. 'Is it the werewolf?'

Adam shook his head. 'Can't be – all the

legends say that when a werewolf is killed, it returns to its original human form.'

'Yes, yes,' agreed Nicolai. 'This not *varcolac*. Just ordinary wolf. Waste of silver bullet.'

Adam shook his head. 'Hardly ordinary. You should have seen its eyes. They were bright green. And glowing.'

Nicolai furrowed his brow. 'Yes, but that does not mean it was *varcolac*. The *varcolac* is master of the wolves. They obey him. He controls them.'

'Wow,' breathed Adam. 'No wonder they were so fierce.'

But before Adam could ask any questions, a slimy voice interrupted. 'What's all this, then?'

The twins spun round to find Stuart Smythe thrusting a large microphone towards them. Behind him, his pointy-faced cameraman trained a huge lens on their faces.

Adam growled, doing a fair impression of a werewolf himself. 'None of your business!'

'Ah, but it is my business, remember?' replied Smythe, lowering the microphone. 'I get to film the werewolf story, while Larry "No Ghosts" Craddock stumbles around looking for non-existent spooks.'

Smythe gave a chuckle, but his smug smile quickly disappeared as Nicolai stepped forward and pointed an accusing finger at the oily presenter.

'You are bad man. You care only about film. You don't care if children get attacked by wolves. Bad, bad man.' Nicolai spat on the ground at Smythe's feet, turned on his heel and stalked away.

Smythe made a face, and flapped his hand at the cameraman to tell him to stop filming. 'Your friend doesn't seem to have much in the way of manners.'

'At least he's honest,' snapped Adam.

'Well, we'd best get you back to the castle, hadn't we?' said Smythe, with a nasty, sly smile. 'Everyone's been hunting high and low since they found out you were *missing*. I'm sure that Angela will want a little word with you . . .'

Adam and Lana felt their hearts sink. Angela was going to want much more than a little word and Slimy Smythe knew it.

This wasn't going to be good.

12

The helicopter came swooping in low over the castle. Beneath them, Adam and Lana could see quite a sizeable crowd gathering on the lawn. As soon as they were in the air, the pilot had radioed ahead to say that the twins were safe and sound. So, although they had flown over too fast to pick out individual faces, they could be sure that Angela and Uncle Larry would be among the welcoming committee.

Sure enough, Angela was waiting, and one look at her expression was sufficient to put the last remaining thrill of the helicopter ride firmly behind them. The rest of the *Fright Night* crew looked pretty cross too. As did Lucian, the hotel manager. But Adam also noticed that the Count was nowhere to be seen.

Only Uncle Larry seemed pleased to see the twins – and even he was in a bit of a flap, shifting between relieved smiles and anxious frowns.

'Thank heavens! Thank heavens you're both safe.' He started forward to hug them, but Angela stepped in front of him and cut him off. She looked ready to tear the twins to shreds.

'This really is the *limit*! The last straw!' she fumed. 'You two have given us a merry runaround. Not to *mention* a scare! Your poor Uncle Larry has been fretting himself silly, while the rest of us have been searching *everywhere*. When there was so much we could have been *filming*! Oh yes, you've cost us very dearly. In time, money and headaches!'

'Now, Angela, I hardly think –'

'I'm not interested in what you think, Larry. I'm interested in what these two troublemakers have to say for themselves!' Angela folded her arms, drumming her fingers in the crook of her elbow.

'We thought we'd be back before you needed us,' explained Adam. Despite Angela's rage, he was curious about what she meant when she said the crew could have been filming. 'What happened? Did you see something?'

'See? Well, not exactly,' admitted Uncle Larry. 'But there was a knocking in the walls of that Haunted Corridor you told me about, Adam, and there's an enormous cold spot on the third floor.'

'Ooh, some noisy pipes and a draught. Sounds breathtaking!' Stuart Smythe let out a contemptuous chortle, but Adam had noticed the man's ears prick up at the first mention of ghostly happenings.

'Never mind that!' blustered Angela. 'There was certainly *something* going on, and we were lucky enough to catch it on camera. But that was when I came to fetch you two. And where were you? *Vanished!* Cue insane panic and frantic search for missing children. And what strange phenomenon is going to linger with all *that* going on?'

'It's true,' added Uncle Larry. 'The ghostly manifestation vanished.'

'Whatever it was, the activity stopped,' Angela remarked impatiently. 'And if I was a ghost, I wouldn't be back any time soon. We may have lost our one and only opportunity to shoot anything worthwhile! An entire trip *wasted* – all because you decide to go off on one of your silly little adventures!'

Adam scowled. He had had enough of Angela's moaning. 'If you're out to shoot something worthwhile, Nicolai shot a wolf that was about to eat us. How about that?'

'Yes,' cut in Smythe. 'Luckily for them, I was filming nearby at the time. But not only did I have to stop work to rescue these two, but the supernatural beast was killed. So now instead of exciting film of a *were*wolf, all I've got is some boring footage of a *dead* wolf – with your kids running all over the picture. Our programme is completely ruined – we might as well pack up and go home. Which, to my way of thinking, means that you owe me some of that ghost footage you shot tonight.'

Angela spluttered like a boiling kettle. 'Excuse me, but I'm sure your special-effects department could turn the children into trees and transform a dead dog into a three-metre-tall werewolf.'

Yeah, thought Adam, in an ultra-rare moment of agreement with Angela. It suddenly occurred to him that if Nicolai had arrived a few moments later, and all that Smythe had caught on camera was an image of two half-eaten children, he would probably have used *that* on his show.

'Anyway,' said Angela, focusing her attention back on the twins, 'it was only thanks to Lucian that we had any idea you had gone off into the forest. At least you had the *sense* to leave a note, Lana.'

'You did?' Adam shot his sister a surprised look.

Lana groaned – she'd been hoping to keep that a secret from her brother. 'I was worried we might get into trouble.'

'Yes, well.' Angela glared at the hotel manager as though he was also to blame for the trouble. 'It was unfortunate that Lucian didn't find your note until *after* you had left. Everyone knows you do *not* go off with strangers. Who *was* this man anyway?'

'Benedikte,' said Adam. 'You know – the man who picked us up from the train station? He's one of the staff.'

Lucian fired Adam a puzzled look. 'You mean here at the hotel?'

Adam nodded and Lucian's frown deepened. 'There must be some mistake. I'm afraid that nobody of that name works at the castle.'

'What?' Lana couldn't believe her ears. 'But how come —'

'For goodness' sake!' Angela interrupted. 'So you went swanning off into the wilderness with some *criminal* who turns out to have been pretending to be a member of staff? This really does take the *biscuit.*'

Adam tried to speak, but Angela steamrollered on. 'Luckily for you, Lucian has promised us that the *real* ghosts will return again tomorrow night at the same time. But for you two there will be no further involvement in the filming on this trip.'

The twins gaped in disbelief.

'Now, Angela,' Uncle Larry piped up, 'you really can't —'

'I can and I will. You are both *grounded.* Now go to your room at once.'

Adam and Lana lowered their heads. There was no point in arguing with Angela. Turning away, they trudged past the assembled spectators towards the castle. As they reached the steps, though, the twins suddenly caught sight of the thin figure of the Count.

He was standing beside the stables, half hidden in shadow. His face was dark with anger, and he seemed to be arguing with someone, but whoever it was was hidden from view by the corner of the building.

Looking back to check that Angela wasn't watching them, the twins crept towards the stable – and gasped. The Count was talking to the ghost of the Romany girl! As the twins watched, he waved his hand in a furious gesture of dismissal. Without another word, the spectral girl bowed her head and floated away into the forest.

'Quick,' hissed Lana, tugging her brother's sleeve. 'Let's go before he sees us!'

But they weren't quick enough. The Count turned abruptly on his heel – and came face-to-face with the twins. Even from a distance Adam and Lana saw his eyes narrow, as if he was wondering how much they had seen.

Lana smiled weakly and gave a little wave, trying to look as innocent as possible. 'Come on!'

As they headed towards the castle, the twins could feel the Count's hard gaze boring into their backs all the way. When they reached the main door, they turned again. The Count hadn't moved a muscle.

He simply stood in the darkness and stared at them.

13

Adam threw himself on to his bed as Lana slammed the door behind them.

'So are you happy now you've got us grounded?'

Adam made a sour face. 'Don't start.' He grabbed his laptop from the bedside cabinet and connected it up to his phone.

'Too late, I've already started. I knew it was a mistake to go off on our own.'

'If we hadn't gone then we wouldn't know anything,' replied Adam defiantly. 'We saw those Romany ghosts back in the forest, and there's definitely something strange going on with them – it was like they were being summoned or something.'

'Well, whatever was happening to them, we don't have any evidence. We didn't manage to film the ghosts in the forest, and Uncle Larry missed out on filming the ones in the castle because everyone was too busy looking for us. It's a complete disaster.'

Adam grimaced. 'Yeah.' He bit his lip. 'Except . . . there's something fishy about the castle ghosts too.'

Lana frowned. 'What do you mean?'

'Well, for a start, how can Lucian promise that they'll be back at the same time tomorrow? Ghosts aren't like buses; they don't operate to a timetable. And what was the Count doing talking to that Romany girl just now?' Adam's brow furrowed with concentration. 'I think the ghosts in the forest and the ghosts in the castle are the same – and the Count is controlling them somehow.'

'But how would he be able to do that?' asked Lana.

'I don't know,' muttered Adam. 'Yet.' He tapped a few keys on his laptop and the video clips he had filmed on his phone started to play back. But instead of the wolf in the forest, the first video was a close-up of Smythe and Angela arguing.

'What's that?' asked Lana.

'It's from the meeting this morning,' sniffed Adam. 'I must have recorded it accidentally.'

He pressed another button and suddenly the scene shifted to the forest. The twins could just about see the dead wolf lying on the forest floor, but the image was really wobbly and most of the recording was an incomprehensible blur. Even so, the twins could clearly see that the creature's eyes were definitely *not* glowing. Unfortunately, Stuart Smythe was right – there was nothing spooky about the dead wolf. Adam sighed.

'Don't worry,' said Lana. 'Remember the agreement Angela made with Smythe? *Ghosts Unlimited* gets to cover the werewolf story. So even if you had a prize-winning close-up of an actual werewolf, you couldn't show it to anyone or Smythe will make Angela hand it over to him. All we're allowed to investigate is the ghosts.'

'I guess you're right,' Adam said. He thought for a moment. 'You know, the Count wasn't around when we got back here in the helicopter, I'm sure. Remember that little gate just next to the stables, where we met Nicolai the first time? It leads straight into the forest. The Count could easily have been out in the forest and sneaked back in that way.'

'So?'

'Well, remember what Nicolai said about "master of the wolves"? The Count could be the werewolf.'

'So he's controlling the wolves as well as the ghosts?' Lana shook her head sceptically. 'What about Benedikte?'

'What about him?' asked Adam.

'Well, where did he get to? He must have escaped somehow. Maybe he wasn't so badly hurt after all. Maybe he was trying to trick us.'

'But why?'

'I don't know,' Lana mused. 'Maybe Benedikte wanted us to get lost in the forest and eaten by those wolves. Maybe *he's* the one who's master of the wolves. Didn't you say that werewolves have superhuman strength? How else could he have got out from under the carriage?'

'That's a good point,' agreed Adam. 'But I still think the Count is involved. Perhaps they're in it together.' He shook his head. 'I don't know *what* the Count is, but he's behind all this somehow. I know it. We just need to find some hard evidence.'

'What, so we go poking around – and get into

even more trouble? We're already banned from taking part in the filming.'

'Exactly. So what more can Angela do to us? Listen, Lana: the ghosts, the werewolf, the Count. There has to be some connection.' Briskly, Adam tapped at his keyboard, doing another search.

Lana sighed. 'What are you looking for now?'

'More information about the Rundek Massacre. I think those ghosts *were* the spirits of the victims. If I can find out more, maybe I'll uncover something that will help us. Ah, yes . . .' Adam's voice trailed away.

'Go on,' prompted Lana. Her brother's enthusiasm was catching.

'It says that Count Ladislau was never punished for the massacre because the authorities at the time didn't care about a few Romany people. He totally got away with it. He was even allowed to keep all their stuff.'

Adam looked up, elated. 'Maybe that's it! Our Count said that he inherited the caravans from his grandfather, Ladislau. So that means they must have come from the people who were killed. The caravans in the stables belonged to the ghosts in the forest – that's the link!'

His sister smiled thoughtfully. 'But where does the werewolf fit in?'

Adam groaned. 'I don't know.'

Lana bit her lip, bracing herself for further adventure and probably another large helping of trouble. 'Well, if I'm right, there *is* no werewolf, but we *do* need to find out what the Count is doing in the stable with those caravans.'

'I say we stake out the stable tomorrow night and see if he turns up. If the ghosts are supposed to be appearing in the castle again, Uncle Larry and Angela will be too busy filming to check up on us. And if Smythe really is stupid enough to think that Nicolai killed the werewolf tonight, then the *Ghosts Unlimited* crew will probably be packing up and leaving too. So whatever we find out, we'll have the story all to ourselves.'

'You know,' said Lana, 'sometimes you're a lot smarter than you look. Sometimes.'

'Thanks.' Adam grinned, tucked his arms behind his head and leaned back against his pillows. 'Now, let's get some sleep.'

14

The next day seemed to drag on forever.

Banned from joining in with the filming, Adam and Lana had to amuse themselves. When they heard that a camera crew was going back down to the village to collect more background material, they asked if they could go along for the ride, promising to be on their best behaviour. But Angela flatly ruled it out.

Things got better after lunch, when the *Ghosts Unlimited* crew loaded what looked like about half a tonne of expensive gear on to their swanky Land Rovers and snaked back off down the drive. The twins didn't see Stuart Smythe leave, but they heard his helicopter roaring away overhead and felt much better knowing that he and his cronies were off the scene.

The highlight of the day, though, came just before dinner. The twins had gone for a quick walk in the grounds when they spotted Nicolai through a gap in one of the tumbledown stone walls.

'Hi, Nicolai,' called Adam and the young shepherd jogged over towards them.

'Going hunting in the forest again?' asked Lana.

'Yes. The *varcolac* is still there,' replied Nicolai. 'I sense him.'

'Well, good luck,' said Adam. 'And be careful.'

'Always,' grinned Nicolai. 'What are you going to do?'

'We're going to keep an eye on the Count,' replied Lana.

'He's always hanging around the old stable,' said Adam. 'We're going to wait for him and try to slip inside and see what he's up to.'

Nicolai pursed his lips and nodded wisely. 'Yes, follow him. Good plan. But find good hiding place. Make sure you are not seen.'

'We will.' Adam and Lana smiled at each other as Nicolai gave them a wave and set off into the forest.

The sun was just setting, blood-red, over the castle battlements. It was almost time for the twins to begin their own hunt.

Dinner, however, was an unpleasant experience.

Angela had the twins under constant surveillance, as if she expected them to set fire to the tablecloth when she wasn't looking. As they were finishing dessert, she spoke to them for the first time.

'Now, everyone is going to be busy for the next few hours, setting up for the ghost watch,' she reminded them. 'I'm not going to be able to spare anyone to keep an eye on you, but that doesn't mean you're free to run around the place.' Angela's eyes sharpened almost to pinpoints. 'If you wish to be involved in future episodes, you will stay inside your room and take extra *special* care not to cause any disruption. Do I make myself *clear*?'

'Yes, Angela,' said Lana, terrified that she might blush and give them away. She just had to hope that the secrets locked up in the stable would reveal such a great story that Angela would have to forgive them for disobeying her.

As Angela marched off to start setting up, Uncle Larry crept over to the twins. 'Sorry you're being left out, children,' he whispered. 'I've tried talking to her, but she just won't listen.'

'Never mind, Uncle Larry,' said Adam. 'We're sorry we messed up the filming last night.'

'Well, hopefully we'll get something even better tonight,' replied Uncle Larry, his eyes twinkling. 'I've got a feeling something *big* is going to happen.'

'Larry, where *are* you?' barked Angela from the next room. Uncle Larry jumped as if someone had dropped a hot coal down his underpants.

'Coming, Angela!' he called. 'You two had better run along to your room now. See you later.' And with that, Uncle Larry scuttled off.

'Right,' said Adam. 'Time to get going.'

Taking care that they couldn't be seen from the dining room, the twins slipped out of the castle and across the lawn. Luckily, not all the outbuildings were locked. Next to the stable, the twins found an old shed with a broken door hanging off its hinges. Sneaking inside, they propped the door back in place and looked around.

It was little more than a lean-to with a straw-and-dirt floor, probably once used for storage. There were a number of old crates and boxes, battered and empty, strewn around. Moving one of the sturdier-looking crates into position under a small window, they could take turns watching the stable entrance.

Minutes stretched into an hour. The twins saw nothing apart from gathering darkness, but somehow *this* waiting was far more exciting than the day they had spent twiddling their thumbs. It felt like they were doing something worthwhile – and the sense that something was about to happen charged the night air like electricity.

Lana hoped that if something was going to take place, it would be soon. Before Angela got a chance to check their room and discovered they were missing. Again. Suddenly, she glimpsed a shadow rounding the corner of the building.

The Count was easily identifiable by his tall, thin silhouette. And, sure enough, he stole up to the stable door. Taking a gentle hold of the padlock, he turned a key and slipped inside.

'Come on,' whispered Lana, hopping down from the crate. The twins crept outside. Together, they edged up to the stable door and listened for sounds of movement inside. Silence.

Moving as slowly as he could, Adam pressed his eye to the gap, taking a peek. 'There's light,' he said softly. 'Candles or something.'

The twins exchanged glances. They each took a deep breath. Then, tentatively, Adam tested the door. It inched open with the faintest of creaks. But there was no reaction from within. Through the narrow gap, the twins squeezed inside, one after another, ducking into a dark corner.

The stable was huge. At least half a dozen caravans, in various states of disrepair, stood in an enormous circle. The Count was walking calmly between them, using a burning taper to light brass lanterns that hung from the once pretty roofs. As each lamp burst into life, the Count muttered a few words, almost like he was conducting some magical ritual.

As the lanterns slowly spread their smoky glow into every corner of the stable, the Count returned to stand in the centre of the circle, sweeping his gaze over the caravans, as though admiring what the light had done for them. Hints of golds, reds, blues, yellows and whites peered through a surface of decay. The rotting wood seemed to have come alive.

And Adam and Lana were no longer in the shadows. Ducking quickly down, they hauled themselves under the nearest caravan. Lying flat on their stomachs amid the straw and the dirt, they peered out between the yellow spokes of a wheel, just in time to witness the next stage in the Count's mysterious ceremony.

'Come to me, I command you!' he intoned. He spread his arms wide – and ghosts began to burst into the stable.

They *whooshed* noiselessly in through the stone walls – or down through the rafters – just like they had shot past the twins in the forest. Slowing to a standstill in mid-air, they floated gently down, shimmering as they touched the earth. White and translucent, they formed human shapes: men, women and children, the light that formed them fanning into pleated skirts and long hair, or arranging itself into headbands and waistcoats to adorn their wispy figures.

There was, Lana noticed, a strange sadness in the shadowed hollows of their eyes. And among them was the young girl whose reflection they had first seen beside the Haunted Corridor.

'I was right,' whispered Adam. 'The Count is controlling the ghosts!'

Whether he was right or not, it was a mistake to speak. For a moment, there was silence in the stables. Then, without warning, the Count stalked over to the caravan and bent down to thrust his face into view.

'You!'

15

'Hey! Leave us alone!' shouted Adam.

He kicked and struggled, but the Count had a firm grip on both of the twins. Surprisingly strong for such a thin man, he hauled them out of their hiding place beneath the caravan, his hands locked on their wrists.

'What are you doing here? Spying! Sticking your noses in where they are likely to be bitten off!' He gave them both a furious shake.

The ghosts watched silently, concern crossing their ethereal faces. The pretty girl from the Haunted Corridor wore an especially sorrowful expression. But she had barely taken a step towards the twins before the Count barked: 'Stay where you are! You will not interfere. I will deal with these intruders myself.' The girl froze instantly.

'Go on, then,' Adam dared the Count. 'Show us your claws! Get on with it!'

'What?'

'My brother thinks you're a werewolf or something,' Lana told him. 'I don't.'

'Whatever you are,' said Adam, jerking his arm but failing to break free, 'I can see you're controlling these ghosts against their will.' He glared accusingly at his captor.

'Yes! Help us!' pleaded the young girl suddenly, and she sounded almost like she was singing the words.

'They are spying little children,' the Count snarled. 'They cannot help you!'

'You can,' said the girl, locking eyes with Lana. 'Help us! Free us!'

'How?' piped up Lana. 'How can we free you?'

'Enough! Be silent!'

The girl fell quiet at the Count's command. 'They are ghosts! They are dead! There is nothing anyone can do for them! And I am not going to let little children ruin my plans!'

'We know all about your plans,' snapped Adam. 'We know you've got some power over these ghosts.'

'We know they're the spirits of the Romany people killed at the Rundek Massacre,' said Lana. 'We saw them at a camp in the forest – around a ghost campfire.'

'Yeah.' Adam nodded. 'And they're the same ghosts as the ones in the castle, aren't they? Somehow you use the caravans to bring them here, then you get them to parade around the castle corridors, knocking on the walls and making it get cold. That's how we saw that little girl in the Haunted Corridor on our first night, and that's what Uncle Larry found yesterday.'

'"The most haunted castle in Romania",' Lana quoted, remembering the colourful brochure they had seen on their first night at the castle. 'It's all for business, isn't it? You're planning to use these ghosts to attract lots of tourists. That's why you invited us here. If your castle appears on the telly, you figure you'll get loads of free publicity!'

'How dare you accuse me!' cried the Count, but his guilty look told the twins they had hit upon the truth.

'Somehow,' reasoned Adam, 'you discovered

that these old caravans came with a Romany ghost or two attached. So you light the lanterns and they all come running. You own the caravans, so you think you own them too.'

The Count threw down their arms like he was discarding a couple of sticks. Turning away in disgust and frustration, he gestured at the ghosts. 'What does it matter? They are ghosts! Their suffering is over!'

'No!' protested Lana, thinking of Fergus, the first ghost she had ever met. 'They're free spirits. They're meant to roam – not to be tied to this castle and the forest!'

'Yes!' The Romany girl stepped forward, taking strength from Lana's argument. 'We should be free! We do not belong here! There are other lands waiting to be travelled!'

'You have to let them go!' insisted Lana.

'No!' There was steel in the Count's eyes. 'I will not allow it! I cannot let you ruin everything I have built here! I will not let you destroy my business!'

Suddenly, the stable door burst open, as though blown in by a ferocious storm. In the doorway stood a dark, burly figure. At first, in the dim, flickering light, the twins couldn't see who it was. Then the figure let out a low chuckle. The sound was strangely familiar but the usual warmth was gone, replaced by an icy chill.

'Well, well. Isn't this a cosy little gathering?'

Baring his teeth in a wild grin, Benedikte advanced slowly into the stables.

'Take seven,' said Angela, with more than a hint of impatience.

It was half past eight and in the castle there had been no sign of the ghosts. To kill time, Angela had asked Uncle Larry to do a short speech to camera, but as usual when he was asked to talk without a script, he had stumbled and stuttered through the first half a dozen takes. Drawing a deep breath, she called, '*Action!*' and hoped for the best.

'So here we are in the corridors of Castle Dragomir. A setting that conjures up images of all manner of Gothic horrors, including, of course, the infamous Count Dracula. The stage is set in this, the most haunted castle in . . . w-w-w-'

Angela threw up her hands. '*Vallachia!*' she screeched. 'It's pronounced with a "v"!'

'W-w-w-' Uncle Larry stared past her. In a sort of faltering slow-motion, he lifted his arm and pointed. 'W-w-w-wolf!' he finally managed.

'Excuse me?' Angela glanced behind her. The rest of the crew followed suit. At the top of the stairs stood a grizzled wolf. Its eyes glowed with an unearthly green light. Beyond it, several others were bounding up the stairs, fangs glinting.

Angela's eyes nearly popped out of her head. 'All right, everyone. Stay calm. That's the most important thing. Don't let them know you're afraid.'

Steadily, the pack closed ranks and advanced along the corridor.

'On the other hand,' Angela reconsidered hastily, 'run!'

Lana shrank away and clung to Adam as Benedikte approached. The last time they had seen him, he had been trapped under the carriage, but now he stood before them completely unharmed. Any sign of injury had vanished – along with his friendly grin.

The Count suddenly stepped forward and pushed both twins behind him. 'Who are you? What do you want?'

Benedikte sneered. 'Of course, you do not recognize me. Even though our families have been linked for more than a century.'

'Our families?' the Count repeated uncomprehendingly.

'My family are all dead,' snarled Benedikte. 'But long ago we roamed these mountains freely.'

Lana gasped. 'Adam, don't you remember what Benedikte said just before the carriage crash about his brothers and sisters living in the forest?'

Adam blinked. 'But that would mean he's Romany –'

'I *am* Romany!' roared Benedikte. 'The last survivor of the Rundek Clan.' He pointed accusingly at the Count. 'Your grandfather destroyed my family! But he couldn't kill me. No, he could not do that. So he fled before I could avenge them. Oh, but I have waited. I have been waiting in the forest with my *new* family for the day when the Dragomirs would return to Wallachia and now, after a hundred years, I shall have my revenge!'

Adam felt his blood run cold. 'What do you mean, *revenge*?'

'My brothers and sisters have taken the castle!' laughed Benedikte madly. 'They will feast well tonight!'

The horrible truth began to dawn on Adam. 'It's you! You're the one that Nicolai has been hunting.'

By way of an answer, Benedikte threw back his head and howled – a terrifying sound that seemed to echo off the very mountains and shake the foundations of the stables.

'My brothers and sisters are coming! Now you will *all* die!'

Suddenly, Benedikte's whole body began to shake. With a growl, he fell to his knees, shaking his head from side to side, like a dog trying to dry itself. When he looked up again, Benedikte's eyes flashed with the same green light the twins had seen in the eyes of the wolves in the forest. He grinned, his lips peeling away from sharp teeth that gleamed dully in the gloomy stable.

Adam, Lana and the Count backed away as thick grey hair began to sprout all over Benedikte's face and sharp black claws erupted from his fingertips. With another ear-splitting howl, Benedikte jumped to his feet. But he was a man no longer.

He was a werewolf.

16

Back in the castle, the wolves advanced as the *Fright Night* crew raced away down the corridor.

'What do we do?' shouted one of the technicians in panic.

'Quick, this way!' called Steve the props man. He whipped back a heavy curtain, expecting to find the entrance to another corridor. Instead, he revealed a hidden alcove containing a figure crouched over a small camera.

Stuart Smythe.

'*What*,' bellowed Angela, 'do you think you are doing?'

'Er . . . Um . . .' Smythe stammered.

'Trying to steal our ghost footage, that's what!' snapped Steve. 'You swine.'

For a second it looked as if Steve was going

to punch the *Ghosts Unlimited* presenter, but luckily for him, Uncle Larry broke in: 'We haven't got time for this now! Run!' And everyone did, scattering chaotically in all directions. With a howl, the wolves gave chase.

Uncle Larry, Angela and Stuart Smythe dashed up a staircase and down a long, dingy corridor, with three particularly ferocious-looking wolves hot on their heels. For a moment it looked like the trio might be able to give the creatures the slip. But then, rounding a corner, they ran straight into a dead end. Ahead of them stood a tall stained-glass window, flanked by two suits of armour. There was no way out. They turned to see the wolves at the end of the passage, growling menacingly.

Stuart Smythe was sobbing like a baby. Grabbing Angela, he thrust her out in front of him. 'Not me! Not me! Eat her!' he squealed. Angela's eyes bulged as the wolves fixed her with their unnerving gaze.

Then Uncle Larry stepped in. Reaching to his right, he grabbed the hilt of an enormous battleaxe and pulled it from the grasp of one of the armoured knights guarding the window. It was so heavy, Uncle Larry overbalanced, toppling towards the slavering wolves. Drawing himself up, he took up what he hoped was a threatening stance, hoisting the axe back over his head.

With a quavering war cry, Uncle Larry stumbled forward, his thin legs wobbling and his wig askew.

And the wolves turned tail and raced away down the passage, just as a bestial howl rang out from the castle grounds.

As Angela and Smythe stared at the retreating animals, Uncle Larry turned to face them, an incredulous grin on his face. 'It worked! I actually scared them off!' He puffed out his chest proudly. 'And as for you, Smythe, you're a disgrace. Fancy putting your own safety before Angela's. Not to mention breaking our agreement. Get out of my sight, before I do something we'll both regret!'

Still clutching his camera, Smythe cringed past Uncle Larry and down the corridor.

Angela stood silent for a moment, as if she couldn't quite take in what had just happened. Then her journalistic instincts took over. 'Right, let's get after them! We need to rescue the rest of the crew.'

'How are we going to do that, Angela –'

'You may have scared off those wolves,' interrupted Angela, 'but leave the thinking to me. There's a *fantastic* story here and I intend to cover it.'

Larry's face fell, his shoulders slumped and he let the axe slip to the floor. 'Yes, Angela,' he said, falling into step behind her.

'Oh, and Larry?'

'Hmm?'

'Well done.'

With a snarl, the werewolf leaped forward, slashing at the Count with razor-sharp claws.

In his werewolf form, Benedikte's whole body was matted with thick hair, and his mouth had grown into a pair of huge jaws, bristling with fangs.

Flinging themselves to the floor, Adam and Lana desperately looked for somewhere to hide. Scrambling on their stomachs through the musty straw, they managed to crawl under a caravan. Peering out through the jutting spokes of a broken wheel, the pair surveyed the scene. The werewolf seemed to be going after the Count first, but the twins both knew that they would be on the menu straight afterwards.

With a growl, the werewolf stalked menacingly towards the Count, flexing its claws. The Count picked up a large pitchfork and clambered on top of one of the caravans, with the werewolf snapping at his heels.

'So now we know how Benedikte got out from under the carriage,' said Lana grimly.

'Can we save the "I told you so"s until later?' panted Adam. 'We have to help them. The Romany ghosts, I mean.'

Suddenly, a voice piped up at Lana's side. 'If you release us, we can protect you from the werewolf.' The twins looked around to find the young girl had slipped under the caravan beside them.

'But how do we free you?' asked Lana.

'The spirit of every Romany person is bound to their caravan. Have you ever seen a Romany funeral? The spirits of our home and all our possessions are released, so that we can take them with us on our journey after death,' said the ghostly girl.

'I remember,' said Adam, suddenly under-standing. 'I saw it on the Web. They burn it, don't they?'

'Yes! They set the whole caravan ablaze. Our spirits are carried away on the smoke. The fire can set us free!' said the girl, pointing.

Adam and Lana looked. Still hanging on every caravan were the lanterns that the Count had lit to summon the ghosts, flames burning steadily inside.

'Of course!' Lana grinned. 'We can use the lanterns to start a fire.'

Adam gave the idea some hurried thought. 'It might work. And it might help us too. Wolves are afraid of fire – werewolves might be too. But –'

With a vicious snarl, the werewolf's head flashed in at them, jaws snapping shut just centimetres from Lana. Adam spun around and grabbed one of the spokes of the caravan wheel. Yanking hard, he snapped it clean off and jabbed at the werewolf's muzzle with the sharp, splintered end.

One stab hit home. The werewolf whimpered and snatched its nose clear. But a moment later it was probing again, growling louder than ever.

'Leave those children alone!' shouted a voice, and suddenly the Count hurled himself from the roof of his caravan, on top of the werewolf. The Count and the werewolf tumbled away. 'Burn the caravans!' the Count screamed. 'Burn them all!'

Needing no more permission, Adam and Lana scrambled out from under the caravan and started knocking lanterns over, left, right and centre. The flames caught easily on the wood and dry straw, licking the sides of the caravans.

But as they watched, a scream from the Count drew their attention. The werewolf barrelled into him, lifting him off his feet, and hurled him through the air. The Count slammed hard into a set of caravan steps, which cracked in several places under the impact of his body. Then he slid limply to the ground, unmoving. Letting out a snarl of triumph, the werewolf turned its glowing eyes towards the twins.

Without hesitation, Adam scooped up a lantern and threw it, hard. The glass shattered against the werewolf's chest, splattering oil and flames everywhere. The creature howled in agony and rage.

Adam sprinted towards the exit. The

werewolf, its fur alight, came after him, but Lana kicked a lantern into the beast's path. A blazing barrier leaped up, the sudden blast of heat forcing the werewolf back. Spotting a chance to escape, Adam and Lana ran for the door.

And stumbled over the Count's discarded pitchfork. The twins fell to the floor, and a ferocious roar erupted from behind them. They turned to see the werewolf, grey coat alive with fire, vaulting through the wall of flames.

It landed at their feet, fangs bared for the kill.

17

Instinctively, Adam leaped forward, slamming into the werewolf and knocking the creature to the floor. He didn't have any idea what he was doing, but he knew that he had to protect his twin.

Lana watched, terrified, as her brother wrestled with the werewolf. Adam was strong for his age, but the werewolf was *unnaturally* strong. The stable was turning into an inferno and the werewolf was quickly gaining the upper hand. Suddenly, someone hurtled through the stable door.

Nicolai.

The shepherd's eyes gleamed in the light of the flames as he caught sight of the werewolf he had been hunting for so long. In one fluid motion, he pulled out his catapult, loaded a silver bullet, took aim . . .

'Wait!' cried Lana, grabbing Nicolai by the shoulder. 'It's too risky – you'll hit Adam!'

Nicolai shook her off. 'No! I will not!'

And with that, he fired.

For an instant, everything was still. Then, almost in slow motion, the werewolf collapsed in a ragged heap. The air was thick with the smell of burning fur.

Adam staggered to his feet, a shocked expression on his face, as the bestial features of the werewolf began to fade away. 'It's turning back into its human form,' he gasped. 'Just like the legends say.' Within seconds, the body of Benedikte lay before them.

'Right in the nick of time again!' puffed Adam as his sister threw her arms around him. 'That's twice you've saved us, Nicolai.'

'Do not speak too soon!' said Nicolai, his eyes widening. Adam and Lana whirled round as, with a shriek of fury, Benedikte's ghost rose from his body. The phantom's mouth yawned wide, a pool of gaping darkness blasting them with rage.

Then there was light. Closing in from every direction, the Romany ghosts were suddenly crowding around Benedikte. As the stable building surrendered to the spreading blaze, the band of phantoms pressed in on him, reaching out as though eager to embrace him as a long-lost member of their family. His spirit was caught among theirs.

'We must go!' shouted Nicolai, turning for the door.

'Wait!' called Lana, pointing beyond the flames. 'The Count! He's trapped!'

'That's right.' Adam too had recovered his senses. 'He might still be alive!'

Dropping his catapult, Nicolai leaped through the flames.

Smoke billowed around the twins, making their eyes sting. Lana squeezed Adam's hand hard. They waited until finally the coiling smoke parted for an instant and Nicolai was beside them, the Count supported on his shoulder. Both were coughing harshly. Then all four of them stumbled out of the stable.

Outside, the twins ran straight into Uncle Larry and the rest of the crew. Angela gawped as Nicolai emerged He laid the scorched and battered Count on the ground, his clothes smouldering slightly.

'What in *heaven's* name have you been doing?'

cried Angela, her face as red as the flames. 'If I find out that *you* started this –'

But Adam and Lana never got a chance to find out what Angela would do to them, because she was interrupted by the ghostly figure of the Romany girl, who floated through the smoke and fire to hover in front of the twins.

With a sweet smile, she performed a gentle curtsy. 'Benedikte is with his family once again. He will trouble your world no longer.' She paused, searching for the right words. 'Thank you,' she said simply. Then she was drifting away, back into the blazing stable.

Adam and Lana tensed, sensing something more to come. Suddenly, out from the heart of the blaze sprang a decoratively trimmed caravan, drawn in ghostly lines on the air. Pulled by glowing white horses and driven by two of the Romany ghosts, it raced past in a blast of ice-cold wind. Another followed in its wake, and then another.

Jaws hanging open, the crew stood transfixed as the cavalcade of ghostly Romany caravans lifted off the ground and soared into the night sky. The beautiful sound of violin music echoed across the lawn as, from the driving seat of one of the caravans, the dark-eyed girl raised her hand in farewell. The night was full of cheers and whoops of joy as the Romany ghosts set off on their travels once again.

Only one thing marred the graceful and beautiful sight – a furious figure just visible through a small window in the back of the last caravan.

His features twisted with fury, Benedikte threw back his head and let out one last blood-chilling howl, as the horses, the caravan and, finally, Benedikte himself faded into the shining face of the full moon.

'My word,' remarked Angela. 'What on *earth* was that?'

The whole *Fright Night* crew was still standing around the blazing stable like a crowd at a bonfire-night party.

'They looked like Romany people,' said Uncle Larry excitedly. 'And were those spectral caravans flying through the sky?'

'They certainly were, Larry, old boy,' said Stuart Smythe. 'Ghosts. The genuine article. Shame you didn't have a camera on hand,' he added, lowering the one he had been training on the stable. 'That lot will make a stunning finale to the next *Ghosts Unlimited*. Game, set and match to me, I think,' he beamed, polishing his fingernails on his jacket lapel.

'I think you had better tell us what's been going on,' said Uncle Larry, turning to the twins. Briskly, Adam and Lana related the story of their adventure, how Benedikte was a werewolf, how he had attacked them and how the Count had fought him off. When they had finished, Adam turned to the Count, who was still weak from coughing.

'You saved us. All the time I suspected you of . . . well, way too many things. You were wrong to be using those ghosts against their will. But I was wrong about you. And I'm sorry.'

'Can I say "I told you so" now?' Lana muttered, smiling. Adam laughed.

'But what about you, Uncle Larry?' he asked. 'Benedikte said that he was sending his wolves to attack the castle.'

'Well,' replied Uncle Larry, drawing himself up proudly, 'they certainly did. They were all over the place! Angela and I were cornered, but I managed to fight them off. Then they suddenly seemed to take fright and raced off back into the forest.'

'Benedikte was controlling them,' said Adam. 'When he died, the wolves must have been freed from his power.'

'Hmm,' mused Uncle Larry. 'That's probably true. Anyway, as they disappeared we noticed that the stable was on fire and we rushed down here.'

'Speaking of which, shouldn't we call the fire brigade?' asked Steve the props man, eyeing the stable nervously.

Smythe clapped his hands together. 'Not so fast. I'm still filming here – I think I'd like to roll credits on these roaring flames.'

'Now, wait a minute!' shouted Adam. And despite all the commotion and bustle, he suddenly had everyone's attention. Bravely, Adam aimed a finger at Stuart Smythe. 'We had an agreement, remember? *Ghosts Unlimited* got the werewolf story, we got the ghosts.'

'Which means,' said Lana, spelling it out to a disbelieving Stuart Smythe, 'that footage you've just filmed belongs to us.'

For the first time since *Ghosts Unlimited* had

arrived at the castle, Stuart Smythe was lost for words. 'But – but – but –'

'No buts,' snapped Angela, taking control of the situation. 'Lana is quite right. Under the terms of our *agreement*, all footage of ghosts is the property of *Fright Night*.'

'But you've got no proof,' sneered Smythe. 'It's your word against mine.'

Uncle Larry's hopeful face fell and even Angela looked a little crestfallen. But the sight of Angela and Smythe arguing had triggered something in Lana's memory. She elbowed Adam in the ribs. 'The extra video – remember?'

'Of course!' cried Adam, pulling out his mobile phone and waving it under Stuart Smythe's nose. 'I think you'll find we have all the proof we need right here. I accidentally filmed the meeting on my phone. The whole agreement's on video.'

Lana turned to Smythe with a grin. 'Let's see you wriggle out of that one!'

Angela held out her hand. 'The tape, if you please.'

For a moment, Smythe stood there, his face twitching. Then, with a snarl of fury, he flung his camera into Angela's arms. 'You'll regret this!' he fumed. 'All of you!' And with that, he stalked away.

Angela calmly surveyed her team, like a general inspecting his troops. 'Right, no time for standing around. Back to work! We've got an episode to finish!'

The *Fright Night* crew jumped into action and Angela bustled off, firing instructions at everyone. But as she passed the twins and Nicolai, her face twisted into a very uncharacteristic shape.

Lana blinked. 'Did she just smile at us?'

'I . . . I think she did,' replied Adam incredulously.

Nicolai looked puzzled. 'She does not smile?'

'Put it this way,' laughed Lana. 'This week we've chased a vampire count, met Romany ghosts and nearly been eaten by a werewolf – but Angela's smile? That has to be the most unbelievable thing I have *ever* seen!'